THE COMPLETE CASES
OF THE BLEEDER

Edith Jacobson

THE COMPLETE CASES OF
THE

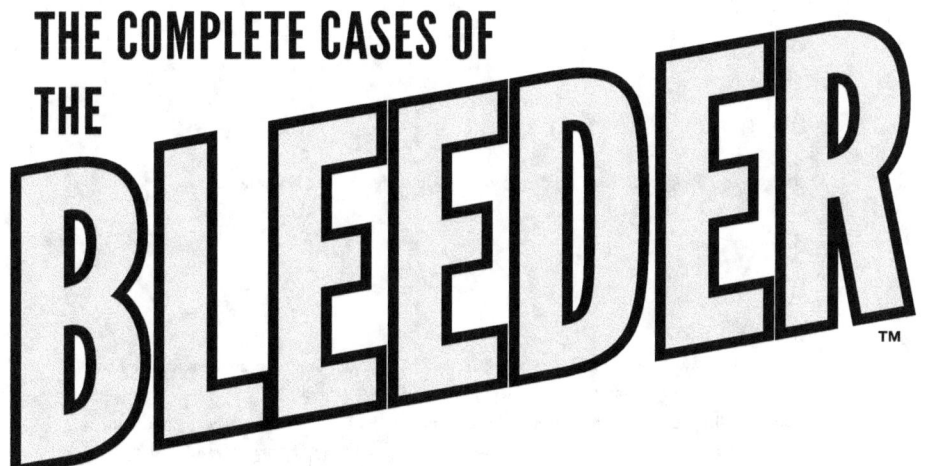

BLEEDER™

EDITH AND EJLER JAKOBSON

INTRODUCTION BY

GARYN G. ROBERTS, Ph.D.

ALTUS
PRESS

BOSTON • 2015

EDITED AND DESIGNED BY

Matthew Moring

PUBLISHING HISTORY

"Living on Borrowed Time; Or, Edith and Ejler Jakobson's Nat Perry" appears here for the first time. Copyright © 2015 Garyn G. Roberts, Ph.D. All rights reserved.

"The Rag Doll Killer" originally appeared in the January, 1939 issue of *Dime Mystery* magazine. Copyright 1939 by Popular Publications, Inc. and assigned to Steeger Properties, LLC. All rights reserved.

"Dead Man—Killer!" originally appeared in the February, 1939 issue of *Dime Mystery* magazine. Copyright 1939 by Popular Publications, Inc. and assigned to Steeger Properties, LLC. All rights reserved.

"Funerals—C.O.D." originally appeared in the April, 1939 issue of *Dime Mystery* magazine. Copyright 1939 by Popular Publications, Inc. and assigned to Steeger Properties, LLC. All rights reserved.

"They Die On Schedule!" originally appeared in the July, 1939 issue of *Dime Mystery* magazine. Copyright 1939 by Popular Publications, Inc. and assigned to Steeger Properties, LLC. All rights reserved.

"Secret Street" originally appeared in the September, 1947 issue of *Dime Detective* magazine. Copyright 1947 by Popular Publications, Inc. and assigned to Steeger Properties, LLC. All rights reserved.

"Coffin for a Bathing Beauty" originally appeared in the September, 1948 issue of *Dime Detective* magazine. Copyright 1948 by Popular Publications, Inc. and assigned to Steeger Properties, LLC. All rights reserved.

"Double Life of a Phoney" originally appeared in the October, 1949 issue of *Dime Detective* magazine. Copyright 1949 by Popular Publications, Inc. and assigned to Steeger Properties, LLC. All rights reserved.

THANKS TO

Joel Frieman, Rick Ollerman, Stephen Payne, Garyn Roberts, & Bill Thom

TABLE OF CONTENTS

LIVING ON BORROWED TIME;
OR, EDITH AND EJLER JAKOBSON'S
NAT PERRY

GARYN G. ROBERTS, Ph.D

"**D**EFECTIVE DETECTIVE"—WHAT marvelous alliteration, what promise the term holds! And, rightfully so.

When asked to define "Defective Detective," fans and scholars often, appropriately, begin their surveys and analyses recounting a very broad literary and popular culture history. The shortcomings and quirks of Poe's C. Auguste Dupin are enumerated. There is usually reference to Sherlock Holmes's seven-percent solution and his other addictions and eccentricities. Even Christie's Miss Marple's old age is noted.

Authors of Detective Fiction and Heroic Fiction learned right away that the "defect" was an essential facet of their lead characters, and an indispensable component of plot development. Siegel and Shuster learned very quickly that comic book tales of Superman required, even demanded, their hero's weakness to Kryptonite. If Superman were flawless, free of any serious maladies, then adventures of Superman would end before they got started. There would be no plot complications—Superman would never be challenged.

As expected, the same held true for all the successful detective heroes of pulp fiction—even before the so-called era of the "Defective Detective" in the pulpwood magazines. Consider the challenges of Nick Carter, the Crimson Clown, the Shadow, the Spider, Doc Savage, Operator #5, the Moon Man, and countless others.

SOCIAL AND CULTURAL CONTEXT

BY THE first half of 1939—the time when the four Nat Perry stories debuted, and concluded—the "Weird Menace" tale was a good five years old in pulp magazines. A handful of publishers had featured these rather gruesome, even humorous variants of Private Eye Detective Fiction and Grand Guignol storylines. Standard Magazines published the "Thrilling" line, including *Thrilling Mysteries*. Red Circle was the most notorious and extreme, and published the short-lived *Mystery Tales*—a pulp, that, in this essayist's opinion, just went too far. The most prolific and successful of these schlock purveyors was Popular Publications, disseminator of *Strange Detective Mysteries, Terror Tales, Horror Stories* and *Dime Mystery*—the pulpwood where tales of the Jakobsons' Nat Perry appeared.

The history of the Weird Menace pulp story formula of the 1930s has been chronicled in a range of sources for decades now. And while it is not necessary to recount that well-documented history here, it is important to note that the Defective Detective found new life in the cauldron of Weird Menace.

The folklore goes that, about 1938, PTAs (Parent Teacher Associations) of greater New York City objected to the wild storylines, abject horror and sexual content of Weird Menace pulps. The "slick" magazine, *The American Mercury,* printed an emphatic indictment of the "shudder" and "terror" pulps in its April 1938 issue.

Pulpwood editors and publishers, promising to change their Weird Menace ways, altered their story inventions (i.e. new elements, twists) so that emphasis was taken away from sadomasochistic themes and replaced with the defects of the private detective. Interestingly, however, defective pulp detectives had appeared as early as October 1937 in *Strange Detective Mysteries.* And, A.A. and Rose Wyn's *Ten Detective Aces* (and its Hersey Publishers predecessors, *The Dragnet* and *The Detective-Dragnet*) featured characters with noted personal challenges and defects that dated back to the late 1920s. Consider Paul Chadwick's Wade Hammond, Norvell Page's Ken Carter, Lester Dent's Lee Nace, Frederick C. Davis's Moon Man, and a range of others with varying degrees of defects.

Again, in a broad sense, Defective Detectives dated back to at the least the nineteenth century. However, the "defects" in late Depression-era gumshoes went to some newly inventive and creative extremes. Beyond Nat Perry (whom we will discuss in a few upcoming lines), there were blind detectives, a memory-losing/amnesiac sleuth, and a range of physically challenged heroes. One was a "crab" detective, so named because he scuttled along on all fours like a crab. There were even allusions to detectives with diverse ethnic backgrounds—including a Native American—as "defective" because of their ethnicities. Of course, today, each of these detective types would have to be justified and explained with different sensitivities.

Now, the truth of the matter includes the following two considerations. First, not all Weird Menace publishers succumbed to the edicts of "moral judgments." Several continued on with no apparent abandon, and even new stories of Defective Detectives still operated in the world of pretty intense Weird Menace.

Perhaps, any perceived controversy about Weird Menace actually accelerated interest and sales in these stories. Publishers would hardly argue with sales.

Second, while some shills of Weird Menace published and thrived with these story formulas well into the 1940s, what probably caused the demise of this branch of Detective Fiction and Horror, more than some moral objections, was a simple wearing out of the once-popular, formulaic storyline. The tales became too conventional, too predictable and could not be balanced with even the wildest of Weird Menace inventions.

By the end of the fourth Nat "The Bleeder" Perry dime mystery, the Jakobsons may have reached a similar plateau with their Defective Detective.

"EDITH AND EJLER JAKOBSON"

EJLER JAKOBSSON was born in Finland, December 6, 1911. Along with his wife, Edith, the English-speaking Ejler made significant contributions to pulp magazine fiction. The couple is often remembered for their short story contributions to Popular Publications' Weird Menace magazines, and to two highly prized one-shot villain pulps (short-lived variants of hero pulps) in 1939— *The Octopus* and *The Scorpion*.

The couple's last name was changed to "Jacobson" for American and English bylines. From the 1940s through the '70s, Ejler wrote and published under his own name. Probably most importantly during this era, Ejler served as editor and essayist for several prominent Science Fiction pulps, magazines and digests including *Galaxy, If, Super Science Stories,* and *Worlds of Tomorrow.* He died in October, 1986. To this day, pulp preservationists and reprint publishers represent the work of the Jakobsons.

THE CHARACTER,

NAT "THE BLEEDER" PERRY

THE ORIGIN story for Nathanial Perry is a familiar one. Nat was a "thin-skinned orphan with the courage dead in him" at age 14. At that time, a victim of a "hit and run," Perry was rescued by Police Officer Harry O'Connor, a "stubborn, gritty, sawed-off little Irishman." Nat knew he was a "bleeder," a hemophiliac—his blood would not clot and a little cut could kill him. O'Connor took the adolescent to the hospital, and provided him with three blood transfusions over four days. The officer reasoned that Nat Perry could never die because he now had cop's blood in him. From that point on, Nat Perry dedicated his life to becoming a police officer—and he found both unflinching courage and a father.

Fifteen years later, at 29, Nat "The Bleeder" Perry finds himself on the trail of the Rag Doll Killer.

"THE RAG DOLL KILLER"

NAT PERRY'S first case, as delineated by Edith and Ejler Jacobson, mutes the traditional details of Weird Menace. The crimes, though gory, are committed "off stage," and the story plotting reads like a modern-day serial killer story. The Rag Doll Killer derives his moniker from the condition in which he leaves his victims.

Lots of conventions and familiar Detective Fiction motifs are found in this story. These include on-going crimes; finding and evaluating clues; perilous, life-threatening battles for the detective; ongoing confrontations between the young, upstart detective and his aging, law enforcing police officer father (similar to, for example, the cases of Steve Thatcher and his police father in Frederick C. Davis's Moon Man stories); and, the detective's final confrontation with the guilty party.

The twist, or invention, of the Nat Perry adventures is the defect of the detective, and his unique vulnerability to certain death. As might be expected, the inventive defect of this detective—the hemophilia—becomes an issue in physical battles. Read how the authors pull Nat Perry through these life-threatening situations. In "The Rag

Doll Killer," Nat Perry's blood disorder is not a major factor. Perry survives by miraculously avoiding dangerous injury. "He felt a little unsteady as he stepped back into the room—there had been so much blood all around him, and somehow, he had not been scratched."

The story concludes with one further portrayal of Nat Perry—this time as a tragic hero (much like Richard Wentworth in Popular Publications' *The Spider* pulp novels). The Jakobsons write, "She [the romantic interest for the detective hero] belonged in the Donegan house, with its sturdy, ancient tradition, and he [Nat] in the obscure safety of his own corner of nowhere."

" 'Good-bye,' he said quietly. He could still see her, a small straight line in the shadows as he rounded the first curve of the highway."

"DEAD MAN—KILLER!"

THE ORIGIN story complete, the next story, "Dead Man—Killer!," really takes off. Immediately, we the readers are drawn into the life of an aspiring film actress in Depression-era New York City. The setting and atmosphere, detailed in the story's header, establish a kind of ghost story and at the same time evoke memories of Cornell Woolrich storylines.

A couple of years since the execution of her criminal husband, Kathi Calvert (stage name for actress Mary Bates), remains haunted by a violent, abusive and possessive husband. As Kathi telephones Nathanial Perry, Private Investigator (with his blood disorder, the Police Department refuses his services as a police officer), Renee (her personal maid, "blonde and pert") opens the actress's mail. Renee unwraps what appears to be an amber perfume atomizer, seemingly from an appreciative fan. The maid sprays some of the "perfume" into her own face. The result of this action, as we read, is horrendous—Weird Menace in nature.

The recurring horror motif, as it is initiated on the maid, takes on some imaginative dimensions as it progresses throughout the story. Along with this recurring plot element is the mystery of Mary Bates's ex-husband. The actress is repeatedly haunted by the specter of her ex, and the question of whether he is alive or dead. While this is all going on, Nat Perry defends his client, looks for and finds trouble relating to the mystery, and defends and holds up his aging, failing police officer father, Harry O'Connor.

The story ends with a return to the tragic hero storyline. The girl

says, "I'll think of you....Why don't you give this all up?" She contin-
ues, "Why don't you take what you could have so easily?" Nat pauses
and considers for a moment, "She was so beautiful." He states, "There
is a man... an old man. I owe him everything, even my life."

"FUNERALS—C.O.D."

THE THIRD installment of the Nat "The Bleeder" Perry mysteries begins with a review and update on the relationship between the
detective hero and his adopted father, Harry O'Connor. Once depen-
dent on his adoptive father, it is now 15 years later for Nat and Harry,
and the roles have reversed—much to the displeasure of the aging
O'Connor. Yet Harry vicariously finds self-definition and renewed
strength in his son.

Aaron Bluff—mean, nasty, ne'r-do-well, former unsuccessful night-
club owner, underworld entrepreneur and thug—interviews police
officers in, of all things, hearses. He is a mysterious benefactor of
Harry O'Connor, and the aging police officer defends his acquaintance's
reputation, even to his stepson. Conflict ensues. The first attack begins
when Nat, driving a black coupe, is first tailed and then passed by a
black hearse. Somehow in his closed coupe, Perry is gassed and crashes
at the side of the city street. The detective is convinced that Aaron
Bluff had tried to kill him.

Along with Nat Perry, readers of the story quickly determine that
the villain of the story is Bluff. However, the curious motif of hearses,
and the bad guy's motivations are the basis for the mystery. Perry's
hemophilia is really not a central element of this Defective Detective
story, nor is the tragic hero ending of the previous two Nat Perry
installments. What carries this story is the mystery of Aaron Bluff's
motivations, the conflict between Perry and his stepfather, and the
role of the hearses in Bluff's deviltry.

The result is a heady mixture of action and adventure, mystery and
intrigue, and Weird Menace/Defective Detective suspense.

"THEY DIE ON SCHEDULE!"

COURTROOM drama begins the fourth and final installment of
the adventures of Nat "The Bleeder" Perry. The physically alluring,
haughty and arrogant "Borgia," Virginia Wilder is on trial for the
murder of her husband, Dr. Grant Wilder. A witness for the defense,

with a seemingly ironclad alibi for Mrs. Wilder, falls over dead as he swears in before testifying. The witness, a cab driver, was to supposedly testify about Grant Wilder's activities the night of the late doctor's murder. Time and place are the issues that should save Virginia Wilder. But, the witness dies from strychnine poisoning, as had Dr. Wilder before him.

Plot twists and turns ensue, and Nat Perry is brought in, by Virginia Wilder's attorney, to investigate the now postponed case. The title of the story reflects the theory in that story that strychnine can be administered in such a way that the death of its victim can be systematically and reasonably timed. Nat Perry solves the crimes, with minimal danger to himself.

DID EDITH and Ejler Jacobson box themselves into a corner? Did the defect of the detective become so dramatic that had the defect been seriously challenged (i.e. Nat "The Bleeder" Perry actually bleeding), the storyline would have concluded the only way it could—with the violent death of the detective hero? The salvation of the hero is found in "luck!" But, the inventional defect of this Defective Detective may actually have become untenable and ultimately compromised the practical longevity of Popular Publications' Nat "The Bleeder" Perry. There was no fifth installment.

SOME 30 years ago, Gary Hoppenstand and Ray Browne edited a two-volume set of facsimile book reprints of selected tales of Defective Detectives in the pulps. The first was *The Defective Detective in the Pulps* (1983). I was honored when they brought me in for the second volume—*More Tales of the Defective Detective in the Pulps* (1985). Gary and I were in our mid to late 20s, in graduate school at Bowling Green State University studying under our all-time favorite professor, Dr. Ray B(roadus) Browne. The imprint for the two pulp collections and studies was the legendary Popular Press.

The idea for the reprints was all Gary's. My new friend and classmate (and long since, lifelong brother), Gary Hoppenstand, introduced me to the pulps back in 1981. I have been hooked ever since, worse than a regular in a Fu Manchu opium den. At that time, Gary had read all the great pulp magazine scholarship, and was even contributing to the same. He probably learned of Defective Detectives in the pulps, in part, from Robert Kenneth Jones' archetypal *The Shudder*

Pulps: A History of the Weird Menace Magazines of the 1930s (FAX, 1975 hardcover; NAL Plume, 1978 paperback)

Gary presented the idea for a reprint project to Professor Browne.

Ray supported both Gary and me in just about everything we did, he was a surrogate father—though he did not like us golfing on Friday mornings with two other professors from the world famous Popular Culture department (Ray was one of the founders of the term "Popular Culture" and he established the Center for Popular Culture Studies at BGSU). Ray felt that Friday mornings were more appropriately spent on writing books. We lost Ray several years back now, though he defines much of who we are and our life goals to this day. We miss you, Ray.

Here's my uplifted glass to you boys, Dr. Hoppenstand and Dr. Browne, Gary and Ray. My life never would have been the same without you. I love you guys. I'd like to dedicate my efforts in bringing these stories back to print to my good friends, Gary and Ray.

THE RAG DOLL KILLER

NAT PERRY WAS A "BLEEDER,"
A HAEMOPHILIAC, TO
WHOM THE SLIGHTEST
CUT OR SCRATCH MEANT
ALMOST CERTAIN DEATH!
SMALL WONDER, THEN,
THAT INSPECTOR O'CONNOR
DESPAIRED WHEN HIS
FOSTER-SON COULD NOT
RESIST THE PLEADING IN A
GIRL'S EYES AND OFFERED
TO MATCH WITS WITH A
SADISTIC KILLER WHO LEFT
BUT TORN AND SHREDDED
FRAGMENTS OF HIS
VICTIMS!...

CHAPTER ONE

THE "BLEEDER" TAKES A HAND

S UTTON PLACE looked like a listless wash-drawing against the backdrop of an East River fog. In front of one of the big apartment buildings, a disappointed group of thrill-seekers had ceased to ask questions of the harassed doorman. From time to time, grim hurried figures in blue uniforms passed into the building or out of it, speaking to each other, if they spoke at all, in terse official phrases. Otherwise, there was a hush about them, and about the place, for death had been an early visitor here.

The Rag Doll Killer, so-called from the condition in which he left his victims, had paid another call. Marilyn Ford was the latest. Once she had been an actress, had married well, and ever-present scandal-mongers had made her a front page sensation, until her quiet life and enormous charities had silenced the cabal. People hadn't talked of her for fifteen years, but now they would talk of her again. She was the third woman to be murdered in eleven months—murdered, apparently for stolen valuables which so far had not been traced.

A quiescent hysteria would arise again among women who had worldly reason to fear the maniac-robber. Husky private investigators would be re-hired, in the capacity of bodyguards.

Nathaniel Perry would not be among their number, and he knew it. He was not husky, for one thing; at twenty-nine, he had a body slim and strong as tempered steel, but there was a leanness and pallor about him that arose from the incurable condition of his blood. He was a bleeder, a haemophiliac. Even a pin-scratch would kill him.

Besides, as he walked past the silent onlookers at the Sutton Place entrance, his concern was not yet with the living. It was with the dead....

The law was in the shambles of Marilyn Ford's bedroom when Nat

Perry entered—the law, in the person of plainclothes inspector Harry O'Connor. He sat there, hunched, as though he were afraid to touch anything, looking hopelessly at the woman who lay in the wide bed, broken and twisted as a child's rag doll. Except that a rag doll is filled with cotton—and the woman wasn't. Perry wouldn't like to remember, even later, the indecent bareness of those pulped vitals.

O'Connor's face went stony when he saw the private detective, but his voice had no stoniness in it—it was harsh and alarmed.

"Get out," he said. His fading blue eyes were shadowed by perplexity and defeat, his shoulders were tired. Harry O'Connor was near sixty. He was getting old. Nat knew it had him.

"Pop," Nat pleaded. "Five minutes."

"No," said O'Connor, but he made no move. The perplexity in his eyes was succeeded by something more personal—tenderness with a kind of pain in it.

They had a nightmare glimpse
of the Cretin's face....

For five years, they had been meeting this way, the young blond detective, and the old policeman. Always, there was increasing perplexity in O'Connor's eyes, the bafflement of a man whose mind is losing its sharpness.

O'Connor hadn't been old before that. A stubborn, gritty, sawed-off little Irishman, he'd been. The only man in the world, Nat thought, who'd have taken on the welfare of an orphaned runaway, fifteen years ago.

A thin-skinned brat of a boy, undernourished, with the courage dead in him, not even normal—that was Nat Perry at fourteen. O'Connor picked him up where a hit-and-run driver left him. Perry hadn't even bothered telling the cop—it was another boy who explained that he was a "bleeder," that any little cut would kill him, because his blood couldn't clot. O'Connor took him to a hospital, and gave him three blood transfusions in the next four days. He didn't moan over the boy, didn't plead; he just said, "Well, you've got a cop's blood in you now—and cops never die!"

AND JUST like that, Nat thought quietly now, he made a cop out of me. It wasn't what he had wanted to do—O'Connor had been as instrumental as anyone in keeping Nat off the force when he tried to join. But fourteen-year-old Nat had really believed those words—believed the curse in his blood somehow lifted, that he could live forever. At twenty-nine, he knew better, but by that time, he'd built his life around the belief. He hadn't been able to turn back.

He had taken certain intelligent precautions. He was listed in the telephone directory only by phone number, with no address given. He kept his skin weathered and tough, developed calluses on his hands, and made a habit of gloves. He didn't hit with his fists, but he had another, more effective method of boxing… and there were people who knew it, and feared it. They also knew he was proficient with a pistol, and ready to use it. They called him the "Bleeder," but they had learned by experience that he didn't start bleeding easily.

He had never been able to convince Harry O'Connor of the value of those precautions—even in the past five years, when Harry needed all the help he could get, just to stay on the force. It was Nat Perry who kept O'Connor on the active list.

But the smell of blood was only beginning to clear from Marilyn Ford's boudoir, and Harry O'Connor was afraid for his foster-son.

She had been in her nightgown, but she had died at noon. That meant, that like the others, she had been unwell. After three such happenings, it struck Perry as more than coincidence.

It was in pre-war days that she'd been known as a famous beauty— but she'd been still beautiful, twenty years later. Again a coincidence— meaningless and puzzling as the first.

The work of a maniac—he looked again at that body on the bed—but a maniac who knew enough to go over an apartment pretty thoroughly.

Nothing clicked. He looked at Harry, saw the facts mirrored in those hurt old eyes. For eleven months, they had set Harry on the trail of a killer who left a pattern as crazy and distorted as he left the bodies of the women he killed.

And then it happened. The meaningless pattern linked in Perry's mind with a conceivable motive. Only a splintered fragment of bottle, with the trade label still on it, spelled that link, but to Perry it was like handwriting, still incomplete, but legible.

He picked it up—with gloves, *Gavreaux, Salon de Beaute*. A thousand women must own jars with such a label, but—there were millions of women who did not. Every one of the victims of the Rag Doll Killer had been a patron of the famous beauty establishment, each had been impressively youthful for her age. And each had been violently unbeautified in death... as though someone were deliberately trying to wreck the beautician's handiwork.

Police had checked on Gavreaux's connection with the murdered women, as they had checked on a hundred similar vague leads—but that was months ago. By now, the connection might be more apparent.

O'Connor took the piece of glass gingerly from Nat, replaced it on the dressing table. "We've worked on that," he said. "You'll find nothing here, Nat. This isn't one of your type things. It isn't brains that's going to catch this killer—because he hasn't any brains himself. He wouldn't even have sense enough to be afraid of you."

Nat believed that. The body was proof of it. But somewhere, behind the sadistic souvenirs of blood-lust, was that persistent pattern. O'Connor must have believed it, too—but he wasn't going to discuss it. He took Perry's arm, and led him toward the door, firmly, but with the bitterness of ruin in his face... a bitterness Perry could hardly bear.

On the foggy street corner, he thought again of that piece of broken bottle, and it seemed to him that the jagged blue edges were beginning to reflect a certain light. Then he got into his car, and drove westward, to a more cheerful thoroughfare.

PERRY parked his car in front of Gavreaux's *Salon de Beaute* on Fifth Avenue. It was a conservative three-story establishment, and in the single front window there was a restrained plaster nude, holding Gavreaux products on her open palm. A mink-coated woman, dignified, austere and handsome, emerged from the doorway, and began a brisk walk up the avenue. She was a living corroboration to the fact Perry had just ascertained over the phone from the woman columnist of an afternoon daily—that Gavreaux's was the only place in town which furnished rejuvenation treatments worth the name.

There was a trace of perfume in the warm chromium gloom of the interior. A girl at the desk took Perry's card, and kept her eyes on it for seconds. When she looked up, her face held a minimum of surprise.

"Mr. Gavreaux's office is on the second floor," she said in a clear quiet voice. "I'm quite sure he'll see you, Mr. Perry."

Perry had not expected so smooth a greeting. The man who nodded to him, from across a walnut desk in the severe upstairs office was hard-eyed, nervous, alert. A business man, from the core out—not one to grant interviews without reason.

Perry began directly. "I believe Marilyn Ford was one of your customers."

The hard eyes grew even harder, as though the man were bracing himself against some shock. "She *was?* What do you mean?"

"She's been murdered," Nat told him.

Gavreaux uttered a short, shocked oath. "That's hell," he said. Then, "You're a detective. I suppose you're working on the case—for whom?"

Nat thought of Harry O'Connor, and replied that he had an un-disclosed client. He felt, as he watched the man across the desk, that Gavreaux could not be surprised again. He was a man who already expected the worst.

"It was this maniac, I suppose?"

Perry nodded. "The Rag Doll Killer. He seems to make his selections purely among your customers, doesn't he?"

Gavreaux's smile was bitter. "He does. The police checked with me on that, last summer. They didn't seem to think much of it—I haven't wanted to, either. Any sane man would call it a coincidence. But obviously, you don't. Otherwise, you wouldn't be here."

Nat Perry agreed.

"I'll talk quite frankly, Perry—you're in business for money, and so am I. That's why I can trust you—I hope—to regard this as confidential. It's getting a little too close. If someone were trying to ruin me—whether out of envy, or any other reason—to ruin this business I've worked like a steel-moulder to build, I'd stop at nothing. If I were only sure these murders involved me...."

Gavreaux swore again, softly. Then he looked at Nat, his sharp aquiline face appraising as a horse-trader's. A rueful twist finally softened his grim mouth. "You may be the man I want," he said. "I certainly want someone—it's beyond me. The police are no good... too much publicity. Besides, they've done nothing. If you get to the bottom of this, and keep my name out of it, I'll make it worth your while. It's shooting my nerves to hell."

Nat was beginning to understand the smoothness of his entry. There were tense lines around Gavreaux's hard eyes, lines that hadn't come there in a day.

But only half his mind was busied in appraisal of the man he had come to see, while the other half killed the question which was already on his lips—the question he had really come to ask. A split-second reaction whirled him to the door in soundless strides. He yanked it open.

"Won't you come in, Miss?"

It was the girl who had taken his card at the desk downstairs.

CHAPTER TWO

THE MAN WITH HALF A FACE

THE GIRL straightened, shook her hair defensively into order, and stepped across the doorsill. She was tall, staunch, straight as an arrow in the simple black dress, with clear pale features and dark, lively eyes. She was the last person on earth, even at second glance, who seemed capable of eavesdropping—yet apparently that was what she had been trying to do. Nat had heard her footsteps, hesitant and cautious in the hall, stopping just outside the door. She had neither come in nor gone on.

Gavreaux sized up the situation at once. "Jane!" His voice was waspish. "I don't quite understand, Mr. Perry. Miss Barnett's my most trusted employee. I didn't know she made a habit of spying on—"

"I wasn't spying," the girl answered, a little contemptuously. She disregarded Nat. "I came to tell you I'll be out most of the afternoon. I'm visiting at Aunt's. She's no better. Will that be all right?"

Gavreaux frowned, then seemed to think better of it, and nodded. The girl turned to go. As she passed Perry, she interested herself in him for the first time. He was startled by a queer ardent plea that suddenly came into her face—and as suddenly died. It was a look so personal that it made him instinctively want to answer her, though he had no way of knowing the question. Then she was gone.

"Who is she?" he asked Gavreaux.

Gavreaux had the air of a man who has come to a decision. "Jane

Barnett—she's been working here for years. I don't exactly get it, Perry; she's almost a full partner. She brought a lot of money into the firm—she has an aunt who's practically subsidized the girl's career. That's Mrs. Thomson Donegan. Jane's also handled Mrs. Donegan's account with us. As you've just heard, Mrs. Donegan's ill. That's all I can tell you, Perry—make the most of it."

Perry thanked the manager, and reached for his hat and gloves. The information he had come to seek had been volunteered.

He was still wondering about the unvoiced plea in a girl's face when he got into the green touring-sedan.

His thoughts stopped as abruptly as the car. He pulled his hand from the gear-shift, and stepped on the brake in mid-traffic, disregarding the angry horns behind him.

There was a neat and minute slice in his right glove. In an almost imperceptible crack in the gear handle, glistened the hair-thin end of a sharp blade. His hand had barely been cut—there was only an edge peeled off the hard callous on his palm.

Slowly, his heart stepped down from the crazy staccato that came to it in danger. He wrapped his left glove around the gear handle, and started north again. It had been no accident. Flimsy enough evidence, and a strong hunch, had sent him to Gavreaux's. This wasn't flimsy—it was deliberately attempted murder. Someone wanted him out of the way, someone who knew his particular weakness.

Someone who wasn't through, not yet. Unless he'd been recognized as he entered, the first person at Gavreaux's to know his identity and presence was the girl.

A trail that began with disembowelled corpses—but the girl shouldn't belong anywhere near it! Somewhere, watching for his next victim, there was a maniac, sadistically perverted... but Nat wasn't dealing with a maniac alone, no matter what Harry O'Connor said to the contrary. No madman would have planted as subtle a death as that in his hand's way.

No, it was a mind clever as any he'd dealt with, a mind the more dangerous because it could couple a madman's methods with a clear intellect. A rotten mind, filthy and cruel, but sane.

A cold inner rage kept him from going to O'Connor with this final proof. Nat was young, with the love of life strong in every cell in his body. But something more than an instinct for survival made him want to be the first to meet whoever had left that blade where he found it.

THE BIG HOUSE hulked on the river's-edge, alone and proud at the fringe of a crowded city. Near the southwest tip of the Bronx, timeless and magnificent it stood, surrounded by a sloping garden that reached from the modern highway to the Hudson. Things in New York grow shabby with age, but the Donegan house had grown venerable, like the Hudson itself.

Nat had heard of Mrs. Thomson Donegan—most people had. Fifty-odd. Enormously active in that vast, vague field called charity. Her name endorsed drives to raise funds for refugees, crippled children, lepers and wayward girls. She had her definite place in the traditions of New York.

An elderly butler scrutinized the detective primly, was pushed aside by a larger and younger man.

"What do you want?" A man of thirty, plump and verging on the bald, with a face uncharted as a child's, confronted Nat. His voice was thin and high-pitched. Nat looked at him without answering, and a stubborn petulance came into the plump face. "Mother isn't seeing anyone," he said.

Opposition was what Nat had waited for. The rage in him crystallized, grew purposeful. He started toward the hall staircase.

"Your mother will judge that herself," he said.

Clumsy, but full of gusto, the male child of thirty rushed at him. Nat caught his collar, and held on. Damn fool, he thought—and then he wondered if the young man could possibly know that the slightest of indiscriminate bruises might be fatal to Nathaniel Perry.

Suddenly the young man ceased his futile struggles. "You've got a gun!" he whimpered. "I see it—you've got a gun!"

"Of course he's got a gun." It was the girl from Gavreaux's. She stood behind them, wearing a small black hat, with a wind-flush just fading from her cheeks—she had apparently reached the house only a little before Perry did. The thirty-year-old quieted and Nat let go of him.

Of the pleading in her face, nothing was left. She was reserved, hostile. "This is my cousin Bob, Mr. Perry. You happen to be in his home. Do you usually begin your visits so forcibly?"

Bluntly, Nat said, "I felt I was wanted here. I came because you looked as though you needed help—and you looked at me."

She stared at him, and swallowed hard. She stood stiffly, hands trembling a little at her sides, as though she were forcing herself to a decision. When she spoke again, her voice was quiet. "Go upstairs, Bob—see if Aunt's all right."

The young man obeyed unhesitatingly. For the first time, Nat found himself alone with the girl who seemed to carry in her heart a secret clue to the puzzle. "Had you another reason for coming?" she asked faintly.

"Yes."

The stiffness went from her, one white hand crossed her forehead. Her mouth quivered. Nat guessed she had maintained a rigid control for a long time, and now she could no longer maintain it, even in her own mind. "I'm sorry," she breathed. "I did try to let you know, when I came into Gavreaux's office—and then I didn't know if I wanted to. What did he tell you?"

"Only what you told me, or tried to tell me. That your aunt was ill."

She sighed, and the sound was akin to a sob. "Do you think it means anything? You don't think she'll... go the way of the others—who were murdered?"

AS FAR as he knew, Nat had been the only one to guess at the recurring pattern which would make Mrs. Donegan the next victim of the Rag Doll Killer. But the girl had guessed at the same thing—guessed or known! What were her premises? Where had she learned, and why was she afraid?

"You'll have to tell me more before I can answer that," he told her gently.

She tried to speak, seemed unable to begin. Finally, she said, "Mr. Perry, do you want to see my aunt? I think she'll tell you, better than I can."

Only a night-light glowed in the neat old-fashioned bedroom where Mrs. Donegan lay. Bob Donegan stood at the foot of his mother's bed, his childish features perplexed and miserable.

The woman on the bed opened her eyes and looked at the newcomers. She was pale, pain-wracked, not young—but she had been beautiful. Her eyes had a dull fever-lustre that seemed to act almost as a veil, and through which she peered intently.

"Jane?" Her voice was faint, thick. Jane walked quietly over to the bedside, taking Nat with her.

"This is Mr. Perry, Aunt Hazel. He's a friend—he's come to help me."

The old lady looked at Nat out of those dully glowing eyes, as though she were trying to fix his face in her memory forever. When she spoke, he had to bend close to catch the words. "Poor Jane... you'll need all your friends. Poor motherless child...." Her next words were for Nat. "I've stood by my girl... always will. Won't back out... till this thing's cleared up. We backed her... several of us. The others died. I'm not dead yet... not all of us dead yet. I won't start a panic. There's always been a devil, but that's no reason... for running away from him!"

Perry's eyes were inches away from Mrs. Donegan's face. Her skin was clear, almost without lines, under the faint discolor of pain and illness—almost abnormally clear for a woman her age, like the skin of a girl.

Only at the corner of her mouth, was the faint beginning of a canker. The detective's eyes were fixed on it—he hardly heard Jane explaining in a whisper, "She means those three women who were murdered—they were all my business accounts. And we can't under-stand—"

Suddenly, the stolid figure of Bob Donegan came alive. He tiptoed toward Jane, touched her shoulder, and pointed excitedly out of the west window.

Outside, a night wind rustled distinctly against a bare bush. At the river's edge, a shape seemed to blur in the darkness, a human shape.

Then, a monstrous shadow seemed to cross the garden, like a harbinger of doom... a shadow, or a living thing. In the dark, it was impossible to know.

Jane looked wide-eyed at Nat. "No one has any business there," she stated.

"Stay here," Nat warned her. He left the room quietly, went down-stairs, out of the house.

A TIGHT sense of danger quickened in his skin as he picked his careful way on the garden's stone descent. It was that feeling he always had on the verge of unforeseeable encounter—that death was always at his elbow, a stern angel with velvet wings and sharp hidden sword.

Sere branches fronded the damp stone walk—he felt their dry tips tugging at his arms and legs. He was sure of only one thing about the man he was about to interrupt in the dark; that those in the house had half-expected his coming. They did not want him; they were afraid of him, and they did not know who he was. Perhaps no one knew that—no one who was alive to tell.

The figure loosening the guy-rope of a motorboat loomed almost directly in front of him. Nat felt for his revolver, and in that instant, a time-worn flag in the stone crumbled under his tread.

Without warning, the loose-jointed figure turned and rushed him with incredible speed. No time to draw—he dodged, and the figure whirled for another try at him. There was a guttural growl of anger, a shadowy bludgeoning of big fists. Nat twisted aside again as the other's momentum carried him past. Nat caught at a flashing wrist with his right hand, twisted his anonymous attacker off balance, and struck him on the head with the calloused underside of his left hand.

In the very moment of impact, he felt a rottenness, a lack of resilience, in the skin that flinched under the blow. An outrageous certainty clicked in his brain.... The man went to his knees, dazedly, and stayed there. Nat Perry used the most ancient scientific method of fighting, and the deadliest. It was born in the Orient, in a civilization more accurately brutal than his own, less careful of human life—and it spared his knuckles from those fateful little bruises.

The man looked up, his face white in the deep twilight, and Nat Perry saw what he had already guessed. His opponent had only half a face. Below the pinched nose, there was only a leprous mess of sores, in which no feature was distinguishable.

"The Bleeder!" he gasped, out of his rotten orifice of a mouth. Then he spread out his hands, showing them empty. "I ain't carryin' a gun or a knife—not so much as a pin on me. I was jest—lookin' for my brother."

Kill or be killed—that had been Nat's challenge to the underworld; that was at the root of his reputation. But the half-faced man squatting on the ground wasn't taking up the challenge as the cold bore of Nat's revolver looked him in the eyes.

Nat had never seen him before, but the man apparently knew him by his synonym in the underworld. That meant a previous encounter—probably before the other's face had deviated so horribly from the norm.

He guessed grimly that this meeting had been planned, but not as it had happened. No, he had been meant to be taken by surprise, just as the slow scraping of his hand from a tampered-with gear-shift had been meant to take him by surprise.

The definite knowledge made him breathe more easily—his skin relaxed. He was about to ask the half-faced man to talk—at the point of a gun—when the rotting features contorted into terror again.

Terror, not of Nat—but of something beyond, something that moved through the grounds with a slimy, plodding sound. The man struggled to an erect posture—the guttural voice, thick with fright, croaked, "Mister, lemme go! Before—"

A girl's scream broke in the open night. Nat saw Jane Barnett racing toward the house as though hell were yawning about her....

CHAPTER THREE

THE DEVIL'S ABATTOIR

SHE WAS not alone—a little behind her, as though he were trying to cover her escape, was the girl's cousin. And closing in on both of them was a thing that bounded like an animal—except that no animal wears clothing and travels on two legs.

The thing reached them before Nat did. With rage and horror, he saw the young man smothered in a foul embrace, saw the girl turn and attempt a futile rescue. Nat brushed her aside, came between her and the thing that had caught Bob Donegan. It was taller than he, even as it stooped over an oddly still prey. It had an egg-shaped head, like a cretin child's, and its mouth was wide in a blood-flecked grin. A shapeless, witless deformity, hulking over him in tattered shirt and faded blue denim trousers—a nightmarish version of the perverted soulless thing that had haunted New York for almost a year—the phantom Rag Doll Killer!

Nat's defense was automatic, a desperate gesture in the teeth of helplessness. He hardly expected it to work—barely thought the thing human. As the cretin rushed him, he slapped an accurate blow to the sloped fuzzy temple—and saw the thing stagger backward, relinquishing its hideous burden of death. He whipped his automatic from its sheath....

Simultaneously, a whistle shrilled at the water's edge, and the thing raced from him like a blooded horse. His bullet whined futilely into the foliage—he ran down the stone steps, sending lead ahead of him into the darkness.

The motorboat was bobbing idly on the black river—they weren't trying to get away. Somewhere in the shrubbery, they were waiting for a better chance—an almost immediate chance—for murder.

He raced back toward Jane, his heart knocking crazily against his ribs. "Your aunt... you didn't leave her alone!" he cried.

She was a shadow, kneeling beside Bob's body. "The butler's with her," she answered dazedly. "We came to see—if you needed help. You seemed in trouble. We didn't know there were two of them. That other thing cornered us in the garden."

Nat stared at the thing that had been Bob Donegan. Throat ripped to the nape, head twisted askew, fastened to the body by one knotted muscle—and soon the gory stream that jerked reflexively from the tattered neck would cease. Bob had died without time to utter even a cry of pain.

Swiftly, Nat got the girl back to the comparative safety of the house, rushed her to her aunt's room. The old lady lay in a half-sleep, mercifully unaware of what had transpired. Beside her bed stood the elderly man who had admitted Nat to the house.

"The shots," he stammered. "I heard shots...." Bewilderedly, he looked at Jane and at Nat.

"Show me the phone," Nat commanded tersely. Before he did anything else, he had to notify the police that a murder had been committed.

The old man led him downstairs, to the front hall. Nat started to dial headquarters, and then stopped abruptly.... The wires were dead!

Nat slammed the receiver down with an oath as the significance of the dead phone sank into his mind. Could his two recent adversaries of the garden have entered the house, found the telephone connections that quickly? And if not they, who had cut those wires? A third enemy—one who worked with his brains, using the other two as tools, must have entered the house earlier.

He snapped at the butler, "See if you can find the trouble, or get help somehow. I'll be right with you."

The girl stood at the threshold of her aunt's room. Without a word, he handed her his gun.

"She's still sleeping," Jane whispered tensely, taking the weapon. "But if it weren't for you—"

A chaotic crescendo of sound, echoing suddenly through the house, interrupted her. The heavy impact of bodies, excited voices, and through it all, one fading cry of agony....

"Stay with your aunt!" Perry ordered. "And if anyone tries to get in... shoot!"

THE OLD BUTLER had reached the source of the sound before Nat did. Perry found him in the basement, crouching over the remains of an elderly woman with blood streaming over her checkered apron. A sea of sick hatred rose in the young detective. He heard the old man snarl, "You killed my wife, you—"

And then the cretin leapt from the shadows, grinning at the old man's agony. Before he could intervene, Perry saw the old man's head circled in the crook of a monstrous elbow, heard the crunching of bone. Protest had been silenced by death—but in Nat's heart, there was another, more furious protest.

A report, an orange streak in the murkiness of the cellar, told him that he had been sighted by the monster's keeper. In the next moment, he leapt for the cretin, who wheeled to meet his rush. Perry's right foot flew forward, caught the cretin in the belly. He grasped the cretin's shoulders, somersaulted backward, and the cretin crashed behind him, on its head—but that head was as hard as the basement floor.

As he leapt to his feet, he felt the jar of another impact which brushed him aside. He reached for the wall to keep his balance, touched the broken ends of wiring on the wall. It was here the phone had been cut.

He dashed after the ghastly pair, terrified lest they reach the upstairs bedroom before he did. There was just a chance that he knew his way through the house better than they did—he made it back to the bedroom where a girl sat by the bedside of a woman who was barely aware of what was going on, and turned the key in the door behind him.

Downstairs, he heard the ominous tread of the strangers' feet.

It flashed through his mind again, that possibility of a yet unseen adversary... for if those two had known the house well enough to locate the telephone wires immediately, why had they not found the bedroom before he reached it? Who had cut those wires? One of the pitiful old pair who now lay united in death in the stone basement? He couldn't believe that....

"You're bleeding!" the girl cried faintly, at the sight of him. She came toward him, anxious, forgetting her own danger for a moment in concern for her unsummoned champion... how grave his danger was, even she did not know.

The white, streaked face of a ghost looked at Perry. He was looking into a pier glass, at his own countenance. He was haggard, paler than usual—and swaths of red blood were drying to black all over him. His own blood? He didn't know. He had been close, too close, to blood, for a long time now... he was tired, almost faint, but there was a desperation inside him that would not let him stop. If it were his own blood, he would drop in a little while, and not be able to get up. There was no remedy. In the meantime, he was all the more pressed to use what time he had. Help had to be summoned....

He waved the girl aside, as she came toward him, his brain working hectically. They were isolated from the outside, as surely as though they had been stranded on a desert island, instead of in a bedroom in one of the most magnificent houses in New York. He had two women to care for—it was out of the question for him to chance worming his way down the outside wall, through the garden, to summon help. He had to stay, and he had to summon the police, with no means of communication.... While, in the house itself, death was coming closer every second.

Jane knew. She said, "You're a brave man, Mr. Perry, but this isn't your trouble. You could get away, if you went alone. These vines outside the window...."

Outside in the hall a slimy footstep plop-plopped toward the door. A loud thud echoed through the semi-darkness as a heavy body hurled itself against the locked door.

FROM the east window, Nat could see the highway, glimmering with its thousand lights... less than a hundred yards away, and yet separated from them by a seeming infinity. He could barely distinguish the separate light stanchions, and the bulbous object on one of them— he had passed that way earlier, knew what the faint bulb signified.

A police call box. It was a thousand to one shot, but he could try. Shots had already been fired on the Donegan estate, and no investigation had ensued... but this shot might bring investigation.

He aimed through the trees, fired twice, three times.

The insistent thud outside the door was repeated. A hinge creaked, the wood seemed to bulge inward. Toward the east, Perry saw a prowl car pull up beside the ruined call box. He fired all but one of his remaining bullets into the air, hoping against hope he would be noticed.

Could he cover the two women, if that door broke down too soon? His eyes met Jane's, found there something valiant and indomitable....

Then, the night split wide open to the blatant sound of an approaching police siren!

At once, the attack ceased on the other side of the door. Footsteps retreated down the corridor. When Nat unlocked the door, there was only darkness. He fired his last bullet after the fading sound of running footsteps.

Jane caught his arm. "Please—don't go yet. Don't leave us alone."

"I won't." He felt a little unsteady as he stepped back into the room—there had been so much blood, all around him, and somehow, he had not been scratched. "You'll be safe now," he told the girl. "You and your aunt—for tonight, anyway. Jane, before the police come, tell me how you got into this. What reason you had for suspecting—what your aunt meant when she said she'd stand behind you."

"You know as much as I do," she insisted.

He nodded. They were alone no longer. Harry O'Connor had come into the room, and after taking one long look at Nat, he said, "I might have known it was you—there's only one man in this town who'd take it into his head to ruin police property."

Jane listened intently as Nat gave Harry descriptions of the cretin and the half-faced man. A queer frightened light came into her eyes—she caught at Nat's sleeve, and cried, "Why I know him! There couldn't be two of them...."

"Know who?" O'Connor demanded brusquely. "You're talking to me now, Miss."

Jane caught her breath, and then answered quietly, "A man who's been coming in for treatments. He lost half his face, I think it was years ago, in a railroad accident. He came to Gavreaux's, to see if they could fix him somehow."

"What's his name?" O'Connor demanded. The old policeman's eyes glinted fiercely, youthfully. "Where can we find him?"

"I don't know." Helplessly, the girl looked at Nat. "I just saw him—never had anything to do with him. Mr. Gavreaux could tell you all that."

O'Connor nodded. "I've sent a man down to fix the phone wires. I'll call Gavreaux when he comes back." Then he turned to Nat. "Isn't it about time for you to clear out?"

"Pretty soon, Pop," Nat agreed. "Here's your man now. I'm just curious. Suppose you try to reach Gavreaux."

The girl looked at him gratefully. Then, as they listened to O'Connor telephoning, he was surprised to see that eloquent, pleading look come into her face again.

O'CONNOR looked up from the phone. "Guess it'll have to wait till morning." He sighed heavily, then said, "We'll find him, though—the boys are watching for him. And when he answers one question, we'll have the case solved." He turned to Nat. "You've done all right. Thanks—and go home."

"I think I'll go, too," Jane volunteered. She looked at Nat again, and her eyes beseeched him to agree with her.

"You'll do what?" O'Connor asked her.

"Please—this isn't my home. I have an apartment downtown. I'll have to be here for a few days now to take care of Aunt Hazel. I just want to get a few things...."

O'Connor looked at her, eyes appraising. "I'll send a couple of men with you," he offered at last. "Keep you out of more trouble."

Nat suggested, "Suppose you let me take her. That's not asking much, Pop." It wasn't, and Nat had done a lot for O'Connor that night... the old policeman looked at the young man and at the young girl, and a half-smile came into his face. "O.K.," he said. "Don't be long about it."

In the green sedan, Jane's uneasiness vanished. "Take me to Gavreaux's," she demanded. There was a fierceness about her—it was like hatred.

"Gavreaux?"

"Yes. I've got the keys to the office. Somehow, I don't feel Aunt's safe, no matter how many policemen stand guard in that house, with that man at large. We may find the half-faced man in the firm's books—without waiting for morning."

Nat asked, with sudden sharpness, "Why couldn't you tell the police that?"

"Because there are other things in those books. Things no one will understand—until the case is cleared up."

"What makes you think I'll understand?"

"I'll chance it," she said, almost grimly, but when she looked at him, there was an appreciative warmth in her face....

The three-story building on Fifth Avenue was dark and empty. Yet somehow, among the covered counters, through the gloomy aisles, Nat sensed a malevolent presence. He kept his eyes on the girl, his hand near his holster, as he followed her into Gavreaux's office.

The pale beam of an arclight outside the window fell on her intent face as she bent over the firm's books. Minutes passed before she looked up. "There's nothing that looks quite like it," she said disappointedly. "Maybe if I looked through his calendar—"

Nat swerved abruptly, as he sensed, this time undeniably, the presence of a third party. Before he could make a further gesture of defense, a heavy body hurled into him from behind—he had only time to make a hard resilient ball of his body as he crashed to the floor. He had a nightmare glimpse of the cretin's face, and a fleet impression of Jane's voice, trying to reach him, as he struck out wildly at the thing hovering over him. Something sweet and soporific stabbed into his lungs instead of air—and then he had only a dazed, confused impression of shapes blurring into darkness.

CHAPTER FOUR

BLOOD OF A CRETIN

WHEN HE came to, he was strapped to a narrow cot, in a small windowless room. A small coal furnace in the corner emitted a fitful warmth and light.

He was alone, but he guessed he would not be alone for long. He wanted water; the humid warmth of the smoky little room was torture. Water, and the clean air again....

What had happened to Jane? If he had only reached her in time.... He could not move. His wrists were tied behind him. He felt himself lapsing into a nightmarish half-coma, as he struggled timelessly toward freedom.

Suddenly a definite sound sharpened his senses, stiffened him into alertness. Plop-plop, down the stairs.... It was the cretin.

Light widened in the doorway. He recognized the cretin by its hulking shape, but there was no way of recognizing the man who stood beside him, whose face was turned to the dark interior where Nat lay. Only an outline, with something in his arms that looked like a girl's shape....

A terse command brought the cretin to a halt. The girl's shape slumped like a sack on the arm of the monster's companion. It was Jane Barnett. She was bound and gagged, helpless.

Again, the man in the doorway turned to the cretin. Nat interrupted, called him softly: "Gavreaux."

The figure tensed, approached him. In the light of the coal-stove, Nat saw that his guess had been correct.

Gavreaux smiled. "Bright of you to know me. I wonder why. You don't look half so dangerous now, Mr. Perry, nor half so able to take care of yourself. Not at all like the intelligent young man I took you for."

"It won't go, Gavreaux," Nat said, his tongue thick with thirst. "Someone else is going to reason the way I reasoned. Someone's going to find you out—you know it. You're scared. You had to have three people killed tonight whom you hadn't expected to kill. It's getting hot and close, Gavreaux."

The hard-eyed man looked interested. "You'd have a hard time proving it."

"No—it's been pretty clear. Whoever committed those murders only ransacked the apartments as a blind. The robberies were too thorough—you planted them to keep the police from noticing exactly what system you followed with the victims. The most important thing you wrecked were the bodies. Faces smashed, organs ripped apart— there was never any need for an autopsy.

"All those killed had been your customers—and they'd all been ill. Of what? No one could tell; there wasn't enough left to diagnose. You've been raking it in for those rejuvenation treatments—you're the miracle man of your field. Maybe it wasn't such a one-sided miracle, Gavreaux—you haven't been the first dealer in dangerous cosmetics. Maybe it was something that killed after it cured— something that rotted those re-made faces. The way it's begun to rot Mrs. Donegan's— the way it messed up your man's face."

Gavreaux laughed shortly. "Is that all?"

Perry gritted his teeth over the thirst and the pain. Words were coming to him slowly. "No, that isn't all. You took in a partner, Jane Barnett, who had the confidence of the right people. From then on, your business was divided into two parts—one run by you, the other ostensibly by Jane. In some way, she brought money into the firm, kept bringing it in—money in excess of the regular fees for treatments. Otherwise, you wouldn't have needed her. And she was afraid to tell the police what she knew, since all signs pointed to her.

"All your victims were the kind of woman who'd share their luck—donate liberally for the purpose of popularizing your wonderful treatments. Perhaps, like Mrs. Donegan, they trusted Jane—put money in her hands for that purpose. Those women died of their own charity, Gavreaux. Once they contributed, they had to die before they found out the treatments were a fraud. Mrs. Donegan intimated that to me in her delirium—she's probably intimating the same thing now, to the police, which is why your time is practically up."

GAVREAUX was still smiling. "That's why my time isn't practically up. You've been remarkably correct in your surmises; but even you must see the fallacy in your conclusions. It's true Jane and her aunt convinced a number of women friends of the philanthropic need of popularizing my treatments—but that was their doing, not mine. The firm's books prove that any money to come in that way, came through Jane.

"I'll be extremely shocked to discover her duplicity, at about the same time the world discovers it, if it ever does. In the meantime, I'm giving her one more chance to maintain her innocence before the world."

"You won't get away with it," Perry warned him. "You're ruined."

Gavreaux paused. "Fortunately, I'm not as afraid of you as my man seemed to be. I actually had to offer him a bonus to tackle you—after he found out he was fighting the Bleeder. I imagine he met you once, before I did—I've never asked about his past."

"What makes you think he won't talk?" Perry asked the beauty operator.

"He won't—and his brother can't. I met the boys right after a train wreck. One of them seemed to be dying. The other was all right from the neck down, but his face was absolutely smashed. I took them home with me, told the less injured one that I could probably make him look fairly human, if he let me use his brother's body for materials to work from. I had such an experiment in mind at the time, and it seemed all right—the man was dying, anyway.

"My patient was cured, but it didn't last. In a short time, the new face I'd made for him by gland injections—glands taken from his brother's body—began to rot. To make things worse, my human factory lived; but he had become a halfwit. A cretin. My patient wanted to kill me then—I persuaded him he'd do better with me alive. Killing me wasn't going to help his looks, and it would cut him off from the only person who could use his services, who knew what ailed him, and who was thereby able to keep him alive. I took them into partnership with me—the cretin, of course, doesn't want anything from life but food and drink. He also has a dependable instinct for trying to get back his own. It's from his body that all the injections ever used in my treatments were prepared.

"And his brother is doing very well, Perry, very well. He has plenty of pocket-money, nothing to worry about—why should he ruin all that by telling what he knows? No one would ever feel anything but pity for the poor fellow."

He picked up an ancient alarm clock from a rickety table in the corner, wound it, set it at midnight. Then he turned to the cretin.

"I'm going out now," he said distinctly, slowly, as he might have spoken to a child, but without kindness. "See this clock? In exactly half an hour"—he indicated twelve-thirty on the clock face——"you can do exactly as you like with him."

Gavreaux stooped over the girl, picked her up in his arms again. She winced, feebly, and then was still. "I didn't mean to stop for a talk, Mr. Perry… just thought I'd drop my pet here to keep you company. In case you're wondering why you've been left alive and conscious, I might tell you that this poor half-wit hasn't any desire to attack those who already seem dead to him."

The cretin's teeth gleamed in a thirsty smile—Gavreaux went out with the girl, closing the door behind him. The coals began to die. There was no bright thing in the room save the face of the clock and the gleaming teeth of a thing that had once been human.

NAT pulled recklessly at the cords that held him, not caring any more whether or not he broke his skin. The cretin snuffled at him, but evidently it had learned obedience in a relentless school—it was giving him his half-hour of grace.

But why? It was not out of mercy that he had been spared for thirty minutes—something was happening, something that thirty minutes was needed for. He pulled frantically—his hands dripped with moisture, but whether it was blood or sweat, he couldn't tell.

It was twelve-fifteen… and his hands were free. The cretin sprang as Nat bolted upright, and the detective hurtled toward the door, ducking under the cretin's onrush. Mumbling furiously, the thing wheeled toward him.

Nat was on his feet, waiting for it. As it came at him again, he slashed at it savagely with the hard underside of his palm. The thing staggered, momentarily, brute anger twisting its already hideous features. Nat struck at it again, aiming his blow where it would do the most good. It was a blow he reserved as a last resort—something that would have snapped a normal man's neck. The cretin seemed not quite dead, but it sprawled on the hard floor, insensible and harmless at last.

Nat found his way up the staircase—discovered he had been confined in a cellar, in an obscure stone house he had never seen before. The alley into which he stumbled was of a type to be found nowhere in Manhattan but Greenwich Village, the oldest part of the city. He had been brought in here unconscious.

Somewhere a clock tolled the half hour… and then there was the louder sound of a police siren. Suddenly Nat understood that half hour of grace.

The police had been *sent*—Gavreaux had meant his murder-tool to be found, to draw attention from his own activities. Half an hour, he'd allowed himself—half an hour's wait for the undependable maniac, who would then have been taken into custody for the time being as sole perpetrator of the Rag Doll murders, to which Nat's body would have been mute testimony.

There would have been no one to tie Gavreaux to the crimes—no one but a sick old lady.

Harry O'Connor was walking into the narrow little alley when Perry met him, Harry O'Connor with his old eyes half-frantic from worry. There were men in blue behind him.

"Nat! You damned fool, I thought you'd…."

"I did, Pop. Tell the boys to go in there, and clean up. You're coming back uptown with me. I haven't time to explain now. I'll tell you about it on the way. I found Gavreaux."

THE DONEGAN house loomed ahead in the moonlight like a big shadow, silent and dark. Harry O'Connor cut in for the first time since he'd heard Nat's story. "Seems empty enough. You were right. Those dumb cops left here as soon as they got the tip-off on that missing link downtown. He could have killed you—and nobody the wiser." They entered the grounds without challenge—the place was unguarded. No voice sounded from road or river—on all sides, the place was deserted.

But in the driveway, in front of the house, stood an empty black sedan.

"You go inside, Pop," Nat said quietly. "It's on the second floor— she'll probably have a night-light burning. You'll see it from the inside hall. I'll stick around outside."

O'Connor started to protest, but Nat had already vanished into the black shrubbery. Wind touched the leaves, making a small music of them. No sound, not a voice or a footstep... he paused a few feet from the spot directly under Mrs. Donegan's window. A dark figure was inching up a century-old vine, and was now almost within grasping reach of the window-sill. He recognized Gavreaux in the moonlight. Still afraid of meeting some opposition in the house, the beautician had adopted second-story tactics. Nat trained his gun on the ascending figure and waited.

Then it happened. The barrel of O'Connor's pistol glinted bluely from the window-sill, and the old policeman snapped, "Freeze, down there—and drop what you're carrying, or I'll drop you."

Gavreaux gave a short cry, paused for a moment on the swaying vine. A dark heavy object fell from his grasp.... Nat snaked toward it, gun still trained on Gavreaux.

But O'Connor evidently had the situation in hand—at a word from him, Gavreaux began to clamber slowly upward. A sudden rustle in the shrubbery beside him made Nat turn his glance.

Then he understood the beautician's easy surrender—for the half-faced man was lurking in the darkness, covering his master with a weapon aimed at O'Connor. A weapon that was never fired—for Nat Perry fired first. The half-faced man rolled over onto the black lawn.

A gasp—it was no more than that—directed Nat's attention to another figure concealed in the shrubbery. Jane... she was still trussed, helpless. Swiftly, he released her. "You can go in now," he whispered. "You'll never be troubled again."

She did not move.

"Nat!" O'Connor's face glared out of the window. His eyes were hard, his voice angry. "Nat, you fool—come on up here! We've got him!"

"You mean *you've* got him, Pop." The apoplectic purple in the veins of Harry O'Connor's forehead were invisible in the darkness—but there was a hint of that quality in his voice as he called to his foster-son, "Nat, damn you—you can't hand it to me like this!"

"You'd better stay put, Pop." The young man's voice was an echo out of the shadows. "If you come after me now, he'll get away. I'll send you help."

A soft hand fell detainingly on Nat's elbow as he started for the highway.

"I owe you so immeasurably much, Mr. Perry—I'd be dead now, if you hadn't come. You've made my life right again."

"It wasn't I," he said. "You had it all, to begin with. Courage… and loyalty. I'm just a dick. This was a job."

"I told my aunt you were a friend," she insisted. "I'll always feel that way. You've been one of the best friends I ever had, just in a few hours. I don't want to lose you. I won't, will I?"

"Perhaps not," said Nat Perry. She had no way of knowing, this dark vibrant girl with her heritage of health and integrity, what curse there was in his blood, what strange companionship he had to offer. Something like a homesickness for the normalcy he had never known made him falter for a second—and then he knew. She belonged in the Donegan house, with its sturdy ancient tradition, and he in the obscure safety of his own corner of nowhere.

"Good-bye," he said quietly. He could still see her, a small straight line in the shadows, as he rounded the first curve of the highway.

DEAD MAN-KILLER!

WHEREVER THE
GLAMOROUS KATHI
CALVERT WENT, THERE
DEATH, GHASTLY AND
RELENTLESS, FOLLOWED
HER. FOR THE CORPSE OF
HER CRIMINAL HUSBAND
HAD COME BACK TO
CLAIM KATHI—AND
ONLY THE INDOMITABLE
NAT PERRY, WHO
ALREADY WAS LIVING
ON BORROWED TIME,
HAD THE COURAGE TO
STAND BETWEEN HER AND
MADNESS....

CHAPTER ONE

THE DEATH SPRAY

AS FAR as Mary Bates was concerned, the February day might have been spent as cheerfully in hell as in her suite at the Concord. If only she could recapture that glowing mood of security that had been hers since the signing of the contract! She was on top, she told herself. She was surrounded by friends and protectors. No longer was she the insignificant and unknown Mary Bates; she was Kathi Calvert now, making a personal appearance tour under the sponsorship of Ed Lorimer, vice-president of Cosmopolitan Pictures, and her pro tem manager. In the next room, there were her personal maid, her secretary, her private physician, and a half-dozen nameless people who had come only that they might further glorify Kathi Calvert in the New York press.

There was no reassurance in the concept. Everything that had happened to her in the last few months, ever since Cosmopolitan "discovered" her, seemed part of a mirage, a dazzling thing with no substance. When had *he* ever been staved off by pomp or protection? What doors had been strong enough against him?

His letter still lay on her desk—one among a thousand letters from cranks and fans, salesmen and crackpots, a letter that could not be disregarded, a summons from hell. "You're still my wife," the bold, familiar scrawl stated. "Nothing will change that. Nothing will make me give you up. You belong to me, and everything you have belongs to me...."

But he's dead, her brain shrieked in tortured denial. Everyone knows he's dead—and no one returns from the grave to claim a woman who hates him!

She seated herself at her dressing-table, hoping to make a reality of the new life by some nervous gesture of grooming she had learned as Kathi Calvert. The face in the mirror, flanked chin-high by piles of presents, stared back at her pallidly. The hair-dress, the tricks of make-up, were new. They had nothing to do with the eighteen-year-old runaway wife of Luke Carman.

But the girl herself had not changed. The same glowing pale face, the same dark auburn hair, the wide green eyes that had been secret pools of terror for four years—all that was as it had been. She was beautiful, and suddenly she hated that beauty. It had made Luke love her. It had been her curse these four years, all the time she shifted miserably from place to place, from one end of the continent to another, supporting herself by catch-as-catch-can jobs, leaving them when she was afraid people might learn her story.

If she could only awake and find it had been a dream, that letter—awake, and know that Luke was dead, as he so justly deserved to be. Awake to another February day in this year of her triumph... or would she? Would she not awake to another year, finding that all between had been a dream? Awake again in a bed of unholy matrimony, in a dreadful white house whose master was the devil?

The walls of her suite seemed to fade away, and she was seeing that house again. Again she was eighteen, and her whole mind was gripped by that ghastly terror of life itself which had been hers as a bride. Again Luke's riders were out on the prairie, spreading desolation and fright. Again she was watching her cousin, Jim Bates, the only one who had dared to care how frighteningly and cruelly Luke had loved her. She heard Jim's screams, saw him die, while she looked on helpless....

GOD, she couldn't go on like this! All day she had faced that letter—and the only comfort she'd had was Ed Lorimer's bland, "We'll take care of everything. Let's just not have any bad publicity."

The girl rose swiftly, knowing she would have to do something or go mad.

She reached for the classified telephone directory, one slim finger traveled down a column headed Private Detectives. Confidential—trustworthy—thirty years experience... the assured smugness of those advertisements frightened her. It would be a feather in their caps, she knew, to be hired by Kathi Calvert. They would make much of it, sooner or later, perhaps sooner—and Luke would know.

And he mustn't know, she thought, forgetting that he was supposed

He brought his right
hand up hard against the
throat of his assailant....

to be dead, that his wife had made any gesture against him. She still
had an older sister, back in Nebraska, with a husband and two kids....

She was about to shut the directory again when her eye fell on a
neat block advertisement. Nathaniel Perry, Private Investigator. There
was a telephone number, but no address.

The reticence of the ad appealed to her. Here was a man who
preferred to remain personally unvisitable, untouchable. He had made
the least possible concession to letting his business be known. He
would prefer not to be recognized by the general public. He was the
man to call.

She reached for the phone.

Renée, her personal maid, blonde and pert, entered the room behind
an armful of packages. "More junk," said Renée cheerfully. "Seems a
pity to throw it out."

Kathi Calvert, born Mary Bates, motioned for silence. Renée
whispered an acquiescent O.K., and began to open the packages.

A calm male voice came from the receiver: "Nathaniel Perry speaking."

"I need a detective," Kathi said nervously, keeping her voice low so that Renée might not be prompted to ask questions. "There's a man who wants me—and I'm afraid of him. You'll find me at—"

"Look at this!" Renée interrupted. She held an amber perfume atomizer admiringly up to the light. "Smells pretty. Bet some poor sucker spent a fortune on it. And Mr. Lorimer won't let you use any of it—say, can I have it?"

Kathi nodded impatiently, and gave her address to Nathaniel Perry, and her baptismal name.

"Who is the man?" the detective's voice inquired with a trace of scepticism. Kathi Calvert never answered. Standing in front of the mirror, her pert blonde head tipped sideways, Renée had just sprayed the perfume into her face.

With the first squeeze of the bulb, a powerful choking odor filled the room. Renée screamed in agony and staggered blindly across the room, her hands clawing at her face. A face, so pink and smiling only a moment before, that was already horribly streaked and blistered!

Acid! Acid in a perfume bottle sent to herself! Kathi's voice was a tortured wail as she ran toward the stricken girl and tried to wipe the acid from Renée's burned face with her skirt.

The door from the next room burst open and a man's hand closed around her wrist. "Don't touch her, you little fool! Want to get that stuff all over yourself?" Ed Lorimer, his dark hawk-like face livid with excitement, stood behind her. Renée's shrieks were only dimly muffled by the pillow she had crowded against her face. Lorimer turned to the open door between the rooms and shouted for Dr. Potter.

Kathi felt suddenly weak and sick, and there seemed to be an earthquake rumbling under the foundations of the hotel. She stumbled toward the pile of packages, those gifts Ed had forbidden her to use, and examined the wrapping in which the fatal atomizer had arrived. A small white card slipped from the wrapping. On it was the bold black signature, Luke Carman. Death had left his calling card.

Suddenly the room was black before her.

CHAPTER TWO

THE DEAD MAY RETURN

NATHANIEL PERRY'S small sedan twisted through the theatre traffic like an agile green worm. He was making good time, he noted with satisfaction—and at the same time, he wondered if he weren't being a fool to go at all. He knew who Mary Bates was—everyone did, who read the papers—and if the set-up turned out to be a publicity stunt which so many of these calls did, no fee they paid him would be worth it.

For one thing, there was the element of publicity itself. In his eight years as a private detective, Nat Perry had stayed alive largely by his systematic avoidance of publicity. He looked, and was satisfied to look, like any one of a hundred thousand New Yorkers. Twenty-nine, tall, lightly-boned and lean, blond, rather pale, inconspicuously dressed in the best of taste, he might have been a young broker or an insurance salesman.

But it wouldn't take much research, if he got himself coupled with Mary Bates—Kathi Calvert—for every newspaper in town to advertise the fact that the slim, blond young man was the Bleeder. Few people would have spotted it, off-hand, for most of those who had brushed against Nat Perry in his business capacity hadn't lived to give a description. By the grace of God, and by his own careful ruthlessness in dealing with the underworld, Nat Perry had lived to be twenty-nine. A scratch could have killed him at any time before that.

He was a haemophiliac, one of those rare individuals whose blood is congenitally cursed with an inability to clot at wounds.

Every case he took was at the risk of his life. He was an extremely easy man, theoretically, to get rid of, and he knew it. He would certainly have had the right to turn down the case of Mary Bates—and yet, if she were acting, she was even better than the advance notices claimed. That scream, over the phone, had been too damned authentic. Something serious had happened, he felt convinced. There'd been a blurred buzz of distant conversation after the scream, and then someone at the other end had hung up the phone with a snap.

A moment later, when he tried to call back, he'd been told that Miss Calvert could not be reached.

He knew, when he braked to a stop in front of the Concord, on Park Avenue, that something *had* happened. An ambulance was pulling away from the entrance; people were standing in little noisy groups, asking each other what the matter was, and two uniformed policemen were telling them it was none of their business and they'd better clear the street.

One of the officers button-holed him. "What's your business here?" Before Nat answered, the man's tired face relaxed into a smile. "Mr. Perry! You on this job? The old man won't like it."

The old man was plainclothes inspector Harry O'Connor, Nat's foster-father, a headquarters man, for thirty years one of the most respected men on the force.

The story of the Irish cop who had picked a dying orphan kid out of the gutter, saved his life by blood transfusions and a lot of sheer will-power, and then brought him up, was well-known among the blue-coats. It was also well-known that Harry O'Connor was not overfond of the fact that his own example had inspired Nathaniel Perry to enter his present hazardous profession. Perry's physical handicap had barred him from the police force—ergo, he'd become a private detective. And Harry O'Connor, who still saw a frail fourteen-year-old every time he looked at Nat, would have moved heaven and earth to get Nat into a safer occupation.

Heaven and earth—but he hadn't moved Nat Perry, for a reason which was not as well-known as other facts about the two. As long as O'Connor lived, Nat was going to stick to his job—and maybe after.

All of that was in the background of Nat's brain as he returned the blue-coat's greeting in front of the Concord. He was glad now, that he'd come over. Somehow, he foresaw, Harry was going to be called in on this. Harry was going to be given responsibilities, problems—and for years, Harry hadn't been equal to them. With a pang of tenderness, Nat remembered the look of bewilderment in those old blue eyes when the going got too hard—and thanked providence that he himself had so far been able to carry O'Connor through, so that it never came to official attention that O'Connor wasn't the cop he once had been.

THE OFFICER said, "If you're going to see Miss Calvert, I'd better take you in myself. They're not welcoming strangers with open arms right now."

Nat accepted the escort, only commenting mildly, "She sent for me. What happened?"

"Somebody sent the little lady the wrong kind of a bokay. Sort of a cross between a stink-bomb and a diamond necklace."

"Publicity stunt?" Perry hazarded. They were in the elevator.

"If that was a stunt," said the officer, wiping his flushed face, "they ought to boil all publicity managers in oil. You should have seen what it did to the maid. God! And she wasn't a bad looker, either."

"Tell me more."

Reilly looked helpless. "Wish I could. A perfume atomizer—that's what they said, but we couldn't find it. Either they're lying, or someone walked off with the evidence. Maybe you can get something out of those people, Mr. Perry, but I found them about as cooperative as clams. That girl knows something she isn't telling."

Perry nodded. He had known Reilly, and trusted him, for years. The man was only a little older than himself, and a staunch admirer of O'Connor. "Stick with me, Reilly," Nat murmured in an undertone. "If you hear anything, don't spread it any further than Harry O'Connor. Maybe we'll get somewhere."

The patrolman shrugged. "Maybe."

No one answered their knock at the door of the suite. They walked in.

Two men were standing in conversation in the flower-studded sitting-room. One was young, dark, hawk-faced; the other elderly, with a stethoscope still dangling from his shoulders. Their conversation ceased abruptly as Perry entered with the officer. The younger man asked harshly, "Got the wrong floor, feller?"

"I have an appointment," Nat stated, "with Mary Bates." His blue eyes met the other man's coldly and steadily.

"I'm her manager," snapped the younger man. He spoke as though his nerves were stretched to the breaking point. "Right now, she hasn't any appointments."

Reilly stood uncertainly at the door. He was a friend of Nat's, but it wasn't his business to see that a private detective clinched with a client. It might even shortly be his business to give Perry the bum's rush and O'Connor would do nothing but thank him for it.

Nat stood his ground. He had been sent for, and until Mary Bates herself told him to leave, he wasn't leaving.

He got his answer. At least it was answer enough for him. From behind another door in the suite came the sound of fists rapping against wood, and then a girl sobbed, "Ed—Ed! Let me out of here!"

It was the voice of the girl who had phoned him. Nat made a swift move toward the door. The actress's manager stepped in front of him, his features livid with anger and surprise.

"You damfool snoop, I'll—" There was a gun in his hand, but he didn't finish his sentence, and his gun didn't speak either. With a swift motion, Nat caught the other's gun-hand in his own, dug into the wrist with his forefinger and flipped back the wrist till his opponent cried out in pain. The gun thudded harmlessly on the thick carpet. Nat turned the key in the lock, and got a first-hand look at the girl whose features had been drummed into the subconscious minds of newspaper readers everywhere.

He had seen pictures of her, but pictures didn't do justice to the colors of her skin, her hair, her eyes. They were like subdued flame, leaping into light. For a second, he stood looking at her, and then he turned to the officer.

"I suppose this lad has a warrant to carry a gun, Reilly?"

"Sure, he's got a warrant," answered the officer icily. He said to the manager, "Don't go waving that thing around, Mr. Lorimer. You came darn near getting into trouble that time."

Lorimer, still nursing his bruised wrist, snorted: "If the law can't even keep strangers out of here, we have to take care of ourselves." He turned to the girl, who had faltered one step further into the room. "Don't talk, Kathi! Go back to your room. I'll take care of everything."

"But I must talk to someone," the girl insisted faintly. Her wide green eyes rested for a moment on the policeman, then turned to Nat. "Are you Mr. Perry?"

Nat nodded, and she looked appealingly at her manager again. "I sent for him, Ed," she murmured. "Please."

A TENSE, unhappy look came into Lorimer's face. Whatever it was that had happened, he was trying to handle it alone, Nat guessed, and he was finding it beyond his depth. "Suppose you did send for him? How do you know he won't ruin you?"

Reilly interrupted. "Perry's O.K., Mr. Lorimer. Besides, it's about time you explained a few things."

Kathi looked at Reilly as though he were a cobra ready to strike.

Perry had seen people look that way at a blue uniform before—one word leapt into his brain. Blackmail!

Lorimer tried to stare Reilly down, and failed. He turned to the doctor and said, angrily: "Go buy yourself a drink, Potter—sign my name to the check."

Potter shrugged and left, not at all reluctantly. Kathi was still looking at Reilly as though he were the thirteenth guest.

"If you trust me, you can certainly trust him," Nat assured her. She looked little and helpless, standing there, in some kind of tailored housecoat, with her green eyes sadder than any young woman's eyes ought to be. Little and helpless, and yet she was a million-dollar investment, with all the safety of a thousand-carat diamond in an open showcase.

The three men's eyes were on her, Reilly's icy, Lorimer's feverish, as though she might by a single word topple the substructure he had built so carefully under his starlet. Only Nat returned the frightened impulse in her voice, as she started to speak, with anything like calm understanding.

"It's my husband," she began simply. "Four years ago, I was married to a man named Luke Carman. It was he who sent the atomizer that—that wounded Renée. That we couldn't find, later...."

"My God!" groaned Lorimer. "I told you not to say—"

"Shut up," Reilly told him. "I don't care if you know every judge in the state. If that girl dies tonight, there was a murder in this room, and don't you forget it."

At the word 'murder' Kathi winced. It was only the actress in her, Nat guessed, that kept her voice as cool as it was. "I was eighteen," she continued, addressing herself directly to Nat. "He was over thirty—but I hadn't any choice. We knew Luke in our town as some vague kind of promoter, though, actually, he was the law. A lawless kind of law. He had all kinds of power, right through the mid-west. He was the kind of man you mentioned in whispers, because you didn't know when one of his men might overhear you. He always had plenty of money, and he always got what he wanted.

"Dreadful things happened to people who crossed him, even in the slightest. He had a band of night riders, who used to loot the countryside with him. There was a young lawyer who tried to form a vigilante committee to capture Luke. He died—and his whole family died with him. Not by the gun, Mr. Perry—nothing as clean as that."

Her eyes grew bitter with memory. "Luke had a favorite trick—almost a trade mark. He and his gang would invade a man's house by night, and in the morning, the whole family would be found dying of acid wounds, all over their bodies.... I had a family, Mr. Perry, and God help me, he wanted something of me. He wanted me to be his wife."

Two things made Nat believe her. There was the fierce sadness in her eyes, a sadness no actress could simulate. It was a sadness that had been years in growing there. And, too, there was an insistent ticking in the back of his head, a reminder that he'd heard the name Luke Carman before. Nothing the girl had said contradicted his vague associations with the name.

"You left him?" Nat prompted.

"I had to—I couldn't bear it. He loved me so much. It was like being loved by the whole force of everything evil in the world. And till two years ago, I never felt safe from him. I kept running away, out of touch with my family...."

"What happened then?" he interrupted.

The girl's voice had a quality of haggardness in it as she answered, as though she were saying words grown old and ugly with repetition in her own brain. "The state of Missouri hanged Luke Carman in Missouri, on April eighth, 1937. Legally, I'm a widow."

CHAPTER THREE

MUSICAL MURDER

NAT WAS conscious of Reilly's short shocked laugh just behind him, of Ed Lorimer's dismayed gasp, and he knew that by all logic, at that point in her story, he himself should have given up. That was what he had almost remembered about Luke Carman: the man was an executed criminal.

"What makes you think he still wants you—if he's dead? Why do you think he killed your maid?"

Kathi Calvert looked at Lorimer, who was making frantic gestures at her in sign language, and then, with a dogged little toss of her head, she drew an envelope from the breast pocket of her housecoat, and handed it to Nat. She said:

"I got this this morning. Read it for yourself."

He glanced at the black, bragging, cock-sure words… *You belong to me and everything you have belongs to me….*

There were a thousand possible explanations, Nat told himself. The letter might be a forgery, the deadly atomizer might have been a crank's trick—and Nat knew he wasn't fooling himself. A thousand possible explanations, but none of them would account for that look in the girl's face. She seemed to remember actual hell; to see it ahead of her, strong as revelation. Kathi Calvert, glamour girl or not, seemed in every way a perfectly sane, normal young woman, and yet, her terror of the dead man was too real, too true, to be dismissed casually.

It was that human element, the strength of terror in her, that made any pat theories mere sophism. This was something deeper, more sinister, than ordinary blackmail. It was an attempt somewhere, by someone, to claim a woman's body and soul.

Perry handed the letter to Reilly. "Get this down to O'Connor at headquarters," he said. "You know enough not to talk to anyone else—tell him I'm keeping tabs. Ask him to check it for finger-prints. Have him wire to Missouri for a record of Luke Carman's prints, and find out anything he can about Luke Carman. Tell him I'll phone back about it, later. And thanks."

"Right." Reilly left them.

Lorimer looked at Nat somewhat more calmly, as though he had seen a match applied to gunpowder and was relieved at hearing no report. Nat guessed that he was beginning to believe that Nat might be useful to him. Kathi Calvert's straight little shoulders had relaxed, and there was that in her face which made Nat certain he couldn't let her down, not if it killed him. Somebody was doing something to help her, what, she didn't know, but something, anyway. It was pitiful, Nat thought, that she should be so grateful for so little. For mere audience and belief of her story…. He asked her for a description of Luke Carman.

"He was stocky and powerful," she said. "That's almost all I could tell you about him. Swaggering, brutish… when I knew him, that is."

"When you knew him?" Nat echoed.

She smiled, wearily. "He had a trick of disguise," she said. "The description they had of him in Missouri was a little different from the one we knew in Nebraska—he had to be that way. Once in a while, a locale got too hot even for him. But I'd know him anywhere. If I died, and they told me I was in heaven, and I heard the angels sing—and then if I saw Luke Carman, I'd know it wasn't heaven. I'd know it was the other place."

Lorimer interrupted, "What about the atomizer? No corpse sent that. No corpse stole it afterwards! Kathi's overwrought, Perry, but that's no reason for believing that a dead man tried to kill her!"

"Nobody tried to kill Kathi," Nat stated. "Lorimer, you wouldn't have been careless enough to let Kathi use any gifts she may have received. You'd have had to expect a few cranks to bother her."

"That's right," Lorimer admitted. His eyes were wide open. "It's not an uncommon practice, though very few outsiders realize it. You mean—"

"That whoever sent the atomizer knew Kathi wouldn't use it. He just wanted to frighten her into contemplating what it would feel like if she had used it. How many people besides you and Kathi knew about the gifts?"

"Only Renée," said Kathi Calvert. Her voice was troubled.

"And Renée didn't know enough," Nat finished for her.

Some of the sharpness left Lorimer's face. He looked at Nat with a mixture of relief and awe, and said, "Well, I'll be darned if you haven't got something!" He would have said more, but suddenly, as a knock sounded at the door, he uttered a startled little howl, and jumped two inches off the floor.

IT WAS only a bell-hop, with a corsage. Nat took the white package, and asked speculatively if Lorimer expected it to contain a bomb.

"No." The actress's manager, grinning a little shame-facedly, took the package from Nat's hands, opened it, and found a card among the orchids. "We expected these. Kathi, they're Cordoba's flowers. I think you'd better dress. We're late."

The girl shook her head. "I'm not going anywhere tonight. I wouldn't step out of here if my life depended on it."

Lorimer was pleading. "Not even if Mr. Perry came with us?" Kathi shook her head again, and Lorimer turned to Perry. "You talk to her," he said. "She can't hide like an ostrich, just because of a letter and a crazy crank. This is a personal appearance tour, and she's supposed to show up at the Star Club tonight. Cordoba's reserved a special table for her, let everyone know she'll be there. Tell her she's got to come, even if she only stays long enough to get her picture taken."

The Star Club, owned by Ramon Cordoba, was at the moment the favored resort of cafe society. Nat looked into the white beauty of Kathi's face. "You ought to go," he said, "and I ought to go with you. You're not in immediate bodily danger. Whoever wrote that letter is trying to break your morale. Sitting here and brooding is about the fastest way for you to help him do just that.

"Besides, I came in here with a policeman and I may have been seen. I'd rather be thought a friend—just someone who'd be at a supper party with you. It'll serve our purpose better. And it'll give me a chance to see who's likely to hang around when you appear in public."

Nat was beginning to get an idea of what Ed Lorimer looked like under normal circumstances. His lively, dark face was alert with the stamp of the idea man.

"Perry," he said solemnly, "if I said anything against you, it was just because I was nervous. You're a great guy. And you know what I'm going to do for you? I'm going to get them to take your picture with Kathi's. That won't hurt your business any, I bet. Foremost Detective Steps Out with Starlet. How's that?"

"If you take any such pictures, or authorize them," Nat said calmly, "I will break your neck with my two hands." He meant it.

Ed Lorimer shrugged. He had thrown a good thing Nat's way, and Nat had rejected it. But Kathi looked at the blond detective with all the gratitude a face can show.

Beauty and the Beast... or rather, the ghost of a beast. As they passed through the lobby of the Concord, Nat's mind tugged at the loose ends of possibility. Anyone might have sent that note—on the other hand, Luke Carman might at present be anyone. Posing as anyone... if he were alive. The girl's attitude about him was almost mystic. She seemed to feel almost that her husband was a disembodied spirit, with power for evil that transcended mere mortality. That was the way many normal people felt, that the underworld was a half-world of sorts... but Nat kept his eyes open for something concrete.

As they passed the arched doorway to the hotel bar, Nat had a glimpse of Dr. Potter, leaning silent and morose against the polished mahogany. The actress's personal physician had had more than he needed and Nat didn't like it. A drunk, even a quiet one, is a drunk. Not that the man hadn't seen enough that night to give anyone the jitters.

Beside Potter at the bar stood a tall, heavily-built man in evening clothes. His back was to the doorway, but Nat could see his face in the mirror. Dark, low-jowled, almost massive except for the weak chin. Nat's mind reacted spontaneously, unpleasantly—there was an oily, almost satanic quality about the man. Potter was inching away from him, in that glassy, silent way, as though the man had been annoying him, but the space between them seemed to be diminishing, rather than augmenting.

Kathi, pale and beautiful in ermine, was walking very close to Nat. He tugged at her elbow, asked in a low voice, "Do you know that man? The one next to Potter?"

She looked, shook her head. "No. Do you?"

That was that. Ed Lorimer walked ahead of them, asked the doorman to call a taxi. Still that dark face lingered in Nat's brain. What did the man want with Potter?

Suddenly a possibility occurred to him. Ed Lorimer couldn't have advertised the fact that Kathi didn't use gifts sent to her by admirers—it would have been bad publicity. Yet someone had known, someone who had either guessed, as he had himself, or who had made it his business to find out. Someone who wasn't Renée or Lorimer or Kathi.

He said to Kathi casually, as they stepped into the taxi, "Your doctor's been hitting the bottle pretty steadily tonight."

"Yes, poor fellow." Her voice was charged with pity. "You see, it must have hurt him—he was terribly fond of Renée."

And then Nat knew.

WHEN they arrived at the Star Club, the Cuban orchestra had just ceded the spotlight to the Name orchestra, which happened to be that week under the guidance of the amiable maestro, Ken Yorgan. Only a few people looked at Kathi, for the people sitting at the small tables were all used to the receiving end of public stares. It was early, and only half the tables were filled. One couple was dancing, but the other guests had come to dine.

It was a long time since Nat had been inside a night club, and he still wasn't sure he liked it. He was vaguely oppressed by the close press of humanity, half of whom wore corsages—it even made him a little uneasy to be so near Kathi and her orchids. It would take just the mildest of accidents with a corsage pin to finish him....

Ramon Cordoba himself greeted them, led them to their table. He had a Latin's grace, and an un-Latin dry humorous twist to his thin mouth—a combination that had brought him where he was.

One glance at Kathi seemed to tell him at once that she was not feeling her best. He murmured something to Lorimer.

"Cordoba's got a table for us at the edge of the floor," Lorimer explained to Nat. "But, he says, if we'd rather, he'll put us a little further back. I think it's a rotten idea. We came here to be seen, and if everything that's happened hasn't kept us away in the first place—"

"Whatever you like. It's your party," Nat answered. He wanted nothing altered, everything to occur as it had been planned.

The couple on the dance floor passed near their table, so that Nat caught the scent of the girl's perfume. She was small and pretty, with a shoulderless, full-skirted black dress and a huge childish bow bound in her long loose hair. Her mouth was very red, very perfect. She looked like a wistful doll.

Near the orchestra, well out of the spotlight, stood a girl in a tailored suit. She seemed in the place and not of it. At the moment she was inserting a plate-holder into a large camera, looking up occasionally at the wistful doll on the dance floor.

Kathi Calvert touched Nat's sleeve. "That's Sandra Benton, dancing. Nellie Jackson's going to take her picture. After that, she'll take mine. And then we can go."

Ed Lorimer frowned reprovingly. He picked up a wine list, put it down, picked up a menu, and asked, "Suppose we stay for dinner; suppose we act human, and forget this mess awhile! A few drinks, a good meal and a little music never hurt anyone."

"No," said Nat. "They never hurt anyone." He'd had little time for drinks and music in his life, and he hadn't much for them now. Still, it was very pretty, the girl dancing there with her tall partner, the orchestra making a soft clatter of a current rhumba, Kathi with her delicate face sitting beside him. Some day, he thought, he might take time off for things like this when he really wanted to—when they weren't just part of a job. He rose from the table. "I'll be back soon," he said. "I have to make a phone call. Try to get the picture over with while I'm gone."

He found a phone booth that afforded him a view of Kathi's table. With his eyes still on her, he dialed headquarters and asked for Harry O'Connor.

The old plainclothesman's voice was tremulous. Excitement did that to it, these days. "I hear you're keeping fancy company. How do they treat you?"

"Fine and dandy," Nat said. "What about that Carman execution? Wasn't there something...."

"You're damned right, there was—and maybe is, right now. They never buried him."

"What!"

"You heard me. Somebody stole the body right after the execution. Some people supposed to be relatives—and later the real relatives turned up. And Nat—"

Suddenly Nat wasn't hearing what O'Connor said. His whole attention was focused on a figure beyond the phone booth. A man in evening clothes was crossing the dance-floor, walking toward a table. A heavy-set dark man, who looked a little like Satan—the same man Nat had seen earlier, at the Hotel Concord, edging closer to Dr. Potter.

HE KNEW that O'Connor had demanded his whereabouts, and he knew he answered. The heavy-set man had almost reached the edge of the dance floor. Sandra Benton was directly in front of Ken Yorgan and she was saying something to him. Nellie Jackson, the photographer, had just flashed Kathi Calvert, and was removing the slide. The man who looked like Satan was at the edge of the orchestra. The slide trombone went to Ken Yorgan's lips.

It was a last static second of tranquility.

Out of the mouth of the slide trombone came choking, strong-smelling death. Acid fumes drowned the perfume and the smell of warm food.

Screams drowned the music. Somewhere a table overturned, and a woman was yelling for her purse.

Sandra Benton, the wistful doll, was dancing no more. Like a maniacal puppet, her dark face cindered and blistered, she gyrated insanely, shrieking wordlessly. Nellie Jackson, the photographer, was knocked down in the rush, and Nat saw the man who looked like Satan grab her camera.

Nat elbowed his way through the stampede, heart thundering, nerves taut, toward Kathi. He had stopped thinking about the corsage pins that might brush against him, as he straight-armed his way like a football player down a field... inches at a time.

A slim vibrant figure was knocked violently against him, trembling little hands caught onto his coat, and Kathi Calvert's voice cried, "Oh God, Mr. Perry, hold onto me!"

Suddenly there was darkness—every light in the Star Club had gone out. Nat felt some violent force pull Kathi away from him. He clutched after her in the darkness, caught the edge of a shoulder-strap, and whirled her into the crook of his arm. Something glinted toward him—the finger-ring on a man's hand. He ducked, missing a crashing blow to the chin.

The tactics he had used when Ed Lorimer attacked him at the hotel suite were peculiarly his, and he used them now, instinctively. Occidental boxing had no appeal for Nat—a bruised knuckle might have been fatal for him. By years of practice, he had developed hard callouses on the sides and palms of his hands, had learned the ancient Japanese arts of self-defense that enabled him, if he wished, to kill a man by means of a scientific blow to the head with the side of his hand.

Now, with Kathi still circled by his left arm, he brought his right hand up hard against the throat of his assailant. A strangled grunt rewarded him. He steadied the girl, kept one arm about her shoulders, and tried to bludgeon an exit.

The rising acid fumes were enough to blind a man, even if there had been lights. It was minutes after they reached the cool blessedness of the open night before Nat Perry realized it.

A man rushed up to them, a man with a frantic look on his hawk-like face, and a thin rivulet of blood trickling across his cheek. He was Ed Lorimer.

"Kathi!" he breathed. "God, I thought I'd lost you." He stopped, and coughed. Everyone was coughing; all about them, blinded, terrified people were streaming out of the Star Club.

Someone among them, Nat remembered, wanted Kathi, Kathi who trembled against him now like a reed in the wind, her orchids crushed, her ermine wrap forgotten, her dress ripped to a rag. Someone who wanted Kathi badly enough to kill for her.

"Run," he muttered. He caught Kathi's left arm, Lorimer caught the right. They hustled her a block and a half before they got a taxi to take them back to the hotel. She never relinquished her hold on Nat's arm. She was like a child in the dark, gripping for safety.

The man who looked like Satan had to be watched. Undoubtedly, he was watching from his own end. *They hadn't buried Luke Carman's body*. Harry O'Connor had said that.

Potter. Dr. Potter had been more than friendly with Kathi's maid, Renée. Potter must undoubtedly have known almost as much about Kathi as Renée did, even of the matters that did not concern him. And Potter had been standing with the heavy-set stranger in the bar.

They were in front of the hotel before Nat felt he could trust his eyes again, and even then, the scent of acid seemed to linger in his clothing, and about the persons of those he was with. Strong, deadly stuff—probably hydrofluoric, one of the most caustic agents known—and specially treated. In the preparation of that acid, there was some clue to the identity of the man who packaged death in an atomizer, death in a slide trombone.... Was that why the atomizer had disappeared?

Death in perfume, death in music. But most especially death striking in the neighborhood of Kathi Calvert, swiftly and without mercy.

CHAPTER FOUR

THE PICTURE OF A GHOST

KATHI WHISPERED, "That girl—that utterly lovely little girl! Nineteen, maybe twenty—and her life's over, because of me! I'd better give up...."

"No," said Nat, his whole tired being tense with the determination that the beauty and the beast remain apart. "You won't give up. I won't let you."

Ed Lorimer seemed preoccupied. He said nothing. He too was tense, his mind seemed to be racing. As they passed the desk, on the way upstairs, he told the clerk to send the first edition of the morning tabloids up to Miss Calvert's suite.

"If they handle it right," he explained, "tonight's mess may be the biggest boost we could get. It'll keep us in the papers for four days instead of one." But he looked a little uncertain, and more than a little sick.

The case would have to break soon, Nat thought, or Kathi would break first. Even if she were not forcibly wrested from all protection, her nerves weren't going to take much more. Once she broke, only a miracle could save her.

He sat down in the sitting-room of her suite with Kathi, half-relaxed over a cigarette. Lorimer went down the hall, still with that tease, thoughtful look on his face, and Nat rose to follow him. Lorimer grunted when he became aware of his company. He pushed open the door of a room further down the hall, a dark room that smelled faintly of whiskey.

"Hope that damned doc didn't get himself too plastered," Lorimer said. "If people ever needed fixing up, we're the people."

Nat, too, hoped Potter hadn't gotten himself too plastered. The doctor was the only one who could unravel all that had happened tonight. His finger felt for the light switch.

Potter was sprawled on his own bed. If he had been drunk, he would never sober up now, and he would never have a hangover. He lay on his back, without even the decency of skin to cover him—for the skin was blistered away.

Lorimer uttered a low groan, and the man's name. Potter did not hear him. Potter was dead.

"**DON'T** tell her!" Nat grated, as they darted back to Kathi. "For God's sake...."

Dazedly, Lorimer shook his head. "I couldn't lie to anyone," he said. "I feel like I was made of water."

"Then go tell the cops," Nat ordered him. "Use the hall phone—and try to look human by the time you get back."

Kathi was crushing her cigarette when he returned. It had taken only that long... the length of a smoldering cigarette, and a man was dead. "There was an apathetic hunch to her shoulders, she had not bothered to repair the disarray of her person. Her green eyes were glazed with fatigue. She was ready to give up fighting. When Ed Lorimer came in, yellow-faced, sweating, she barely looked at him. She pointed to a table. "Your papers came, Ed. I don't want to see them."

There was reason enough, Nat thought. The edition, which couldn't have been on the streets for more than minutes, screamed blackly: DEBUTANTE SLAIN AT STAR CLUB! Nat stood beside Lorimer as he turned the first page for the story.

Pictures—plenty of pictures. A picture of Kathi.... Suddenly Nat felt the muscles of his stomach tightening. A picture of Kathi Calvert, purporting to be of that evening at the Star Club... and yet it was not Kathi as she had looked tonight! That wasn't the dress she had worn; the dress which hung on her now like a torn rag!

Kathi seemed to sense the momentary rigidity of his attention. She rose, snatched the tabloid from his hand. She looked at the picture, and the paper dropped from her hands. In hell, the damned must look as Kathi looked that minute.... It wasn't the dress. She hadn't even seemed to notice that.

"It's Luke," she whispered. *"He was right there*—right behind me!"

Again, Nat stared at the picture, appalled at what it had done to Kathi. There was a face, right over her shoulder; a man's face, blurred as though the camera had focused at a point a few feet in front of him. Luke Carman, the man Kathi would have recognized in hell....

"Who's the night-club photographer for this paper?" he asked Lorimer.

"The Jackson girl—Nellie Jackson. You saw her there tonight."

"And I'm going to see her again tonight," Nat said. No, he couldn't be wrong. He had seen it, actually, in those last seconds before the acid fumes blinded him. Nellie Jackson had just finished taking her picture of Kathi, and then Mr. Satan had grabbed her camera.

Before he reached the door, someone opened it from the other side, and walked straight toward him. An old man, with tiny lines around his narrowed blue eyes; a man with slow steady step; broad, stoop-shouldered. He was Harry O'Connor.

"Come with me, Pop," Nat urged him. "I've got to get downtown. Right away."

Harry O'Connor looked about the luxurious sitting-room, at the slim, frightened figure of Kathi Calvert on the couch, at the sick face of Ed Lorimer. He said slowly, "Maybe you better not go any more places, Nat. You don't seem to bring any luck tonight, wherever you show up."

"You followed me from the Star Club?" Nat guessed.

"Yeah. I followed you. And a fine trail you left. A damned shambles, that's what." He turned to Lorimer. "That little bit of murder down the hall—I suppose it belongs to your party?"

"Yes," Lorimer murmured miserably. "It does. Who are you?"

Harry exposed his badge briefly. His blue eyes were still hard on Nat. There was fury in them. "I guess you know," he said, "that I'm supposed to find out all about what happened at the Star Club. Maybe I'm getting kind of old to be tracking down the side-lines on cafe society, but when these kids get themselves murdered, it's my job. I thought I'd tell you that, Nat. My job. Not yours. Understand?"

Nat understood only too well. And he knew again, as he had known for the past five years, that Harry needed him desperately. Somewhere behind the anger, deep as the deep-rooted love that made him afraid of any danger that threatened his foster-son, there was a bewildered old law-dog in Harry O'Connor. Harry would never give up. He would stumble stubbornly into a death-trap, his old eyes fixed half-comprehendingly ahead of him, before he gave up... and there were plenty of death-traps around tonight, for anyone who stuck his nose into the Star Club murder!

"Pop," Nat pleaded again, with a fervor that twisted his voice a little, "the next stop is the Globe office. A girl named Nellie Jackson. It's a rush order. You've got to believe me. You've got to take my word for it, this is the McCoy. And we're going together."

The anger faded a little from O'Connor's eyes. "O.K.," he grunted. "But don't try to give me the slip. Homicide's busy on that stiff down the hall.... How about the lady here? Is she hurt?"

"No," said Nat. "Just upset." Nat turned to Lorimer. "You've got a gun. If anything happens to Kathi I'll take it out of your hide."

"Sa-ay! Who's paying who around here, anyway?"

Nat didn't answer. He was out in the hall with O'Connor.

THE DAY had been warm, but it was still February. As they drove downtown, Nat said:

"What about those finger-prints, Pop? On the letter I sent to you with Reilly?"

Harry's face grew serious. "That's what I was going to tell you, on the phone, when you cut me short. You've really got something there. I didn't even have to wire as far as Missouri. The punk's got a New York record a mile long. Record ended in 1928. After that he must have gone west. But the prints on the letter check with this Luke's."

"Check?"

"You heard me."

Nat was silent. Then he said, "But they hanged him two years ago."

"That's right," Harry agreed. He sighed. "I can't make it out. Maybe it calls for a spiritualist, not a cop."

Maybe—maybe not! That dim nagging memory he had had when Kathi first mentioned Luke Carman's name returned. The man *must* be alive. They'd never buried his body.... Suddenly he remembered—not what he had been trying to think of, but something else. It was fantastic. But not as fantastic as a dead man claiming a living bride!

Tempering the excitement in him, he asked, "Pop, did you happen to read a story about a Canadian hangman who bungled? He had to execute a woman, and she'd put on fifty pounds in jail. The hangman didn't account for the increase in weight, and when he sprang the noose, she jerked so hard her head rolled off. Pop, did you read it?"

Harry O'Connor winced. "I do better things with my spare time," he said.

"Suppose it happened the other way. Suppose a person awaiting execution lost fifty pounds, instead of gaining them. Suppose the hangman didn't take account of it. He'd simply fail to break the prisoner's neck."

Harry O'Connor looked at Nat for a long time. Then he said, "You mean we're looking for—"

"A thin man," Nat finished. "Of course, he's had two years to put that weight back on; but if he's smart, he hasn't done it."

The Globe Building reared ahead of them, a modern monster at the ramshackle edge of the waterfront.

Nat brought the green sedan to a stop, a few yards away from the entrance. He had found, on occasion, that it was bad business to advertise his presence anywhere by leaving his car parked outside, but now, he couldn't help it.

Harry's badge got them quickly past an office boy. In a corner of the night city room, they found the girl photographer, Nellie Jackson. She squinted up at them over a paper container of coffee. She had a black eye.

"They treated you a little rough tonight," Nat sympathized. "How'd you get your camera back?"

"I beg your pardon?" The girl looked small, fragile, in the tailored suit, at first glance—and then you saw the firm stubbornness of her chin, the breadth and hardness of her shoulders under the tweed.

"I asked how you got your camera back? Someone grabbed it from you at the Star Club, right after you took a picture of Kathi Calvert with it—and yet, the first edition on the streets had a picture of Kathi in it. A rather remarkable picture. How come?"

Nellie Jackson said something very definite to the effect that she didn't make a habit of talking to strangers.

Harry O'Connor pulled back his lapel. "You're talking to the law," he said grimly. "A kid was killed at the Star Club tonight. I think you'd better answer questions."

Even with the shiner, she saw the badge plainly enough. She put down her coffee, and said, "All right. I don't know much, but I'll try to help."

"Good girl," Nat observed. "Tell me this: did the same man who grabbed your camera give it back to you?"

She nodded.

"Have you ever seen him before?"

Nellie Jackson laughed nervously. "Sure. He's been around the town for a few weeks. Once he bought me a drink. It was nice. A girl gets tired of seeing everybody else have all the fun."

"Why did he buy you the drink?"

"I did him a favor. He seemed to have sort of a crush on the Calvert girl. That's nothing. All the men do, though I don't know why. He bought me a drink, and so I gave him a print of a picture I'd just taken. A picture of Kathi Calvert. Nobody missed that print. We've got plenty."

"Do you know this man's name?"

Nellie Jackson managed to look dignified, even with the black eye. "Mister, I wouldn't want to know the people who play in the places I work."

Nat believed her. "Did you develop that picture in your camera tonight?"

She shook her head. "That's out of my line. The boys take care of that end."

"You haven't even seen the picture?"

Again she shook her head.

"When you get around to it, try to take a look," Nat advised her. "It may cure you of drinking with strangers for good."

Nellie Jackson stood bolt upright. "Wait a minute! What's the angle?"

The two men did not answer her. They were on their way out.

CHAPTER FIVE

DEATH'S LITTLE JOKE

IT WAS as simple as that, Nat ruminated bitterly. His Mr. Satan had stolen a negative of Kathi, superimposed it onto another, older picture, which included the face of a man Kathi would recognize as Luke Carman. That melee at the Star Club had been planned deliberately, to give him an opportunity to switch plates in Nellie Jackson's camera. He had done all that, simply by buying a girl a drink.

By buying a girl a drink, and by planting his devilish acid in a slide trombone. The latter maneuver was a little harder to explain—but its effects were apparent. That picture had almost done the trick; almost demoralized Kathi completely. Maybe there wasn't even an *almost*. It would be good, Nat thought, to be able to tell her the picture was a fake.

His mind turned again to what Harry had told him about Luke Carman. He was convinced now that the man was as alive as he was.

A man was standing on the sidewalk, looking at Nat's car. Something in the hunched power of his shoulders under the overcoat made Nat break into a run as he approached, but it was the wrong gesture, he realized at once. Warned by the clatter of footsteps, the man looked up hurriedly, darted toward the corner. A car sailed up the avenue— paused—a sedan door opened long enough to admit a passenger.

Harry O'Connor's shoulders hit the back of the seat as Nat raced his own car into a perkily swift pursuit.

"We're following that car—if we follow it into the river!" Nat snapped.

The passenger who had been taken on at the corner, the man who had been waiting so attentively for Nat's exit from the Globe building, was the man who looked like Satan.

IT WAS LATE. Seventh Avenue, was broad and empty. The buff sedan was setting a fast pace, dashing heedlessly through red lights. Nat stamped on his accelerator, kept it in sight.

O'Connor drew his revolver, aimed at the flying wheels a hundred yards ahead. As his finger moved, the car ahead made a tortured left turn on two wheels into a side-street, and the bullet slapped against concrete, ricochetted forward, riding the pavement in the gutter.

Nat's mouth was set in a stiff line as he rounded the corner and saw the buff sedan nearing the next avenue. A sharp, bright flash blossomed from its rear windows and died at the sound of gunfire. They were answering O'Connor's attack. Nat swerved wildly, out of the bullet's reach, caromed back to keel.

Somewhere behind him, on the street, he heard a wail, like a wounded child's—that bullet had found a random mark, taken its toll in innocent blood.

Harry heard the wail, too. Grimly he pocketed his own gun. The buff sedan was an uncertain target, and if another bullet ricochetted, even a cop's bullet, there were other kids it might hit.... Damn them, Nat muttered under his breath, damn them to hell. They were going sixty now, seventy... still the buff sedan kept its lead on the green one. Where were the traffic cops?

Up the West Side Highway, the chase went on. Somewhere, on this traveled expanse, there had to be a cop.

Jersey lights flickered and blinked to the west. They had traveled half the length of Manhattan islands. Was it going to be a contest between the fullness of their gas tanks?

At the Hundred Twenty-fifth Street exit, the buff car turned off, Nat tailing it. Crosstown, eastward toward Harlem, but now the pace was slower, the traffic heavy. At Eighth Avenue, the trail dipped abruptly south, then east again.

The buff car pulled to a halt in front of a dark store front. A figure scurried across the pavement. Nat braked abruptly, leapt out, with Harry O'Connor.

They burst through the door, threaded the black interior with flashlights.

Almost at his elbow, Nat heard a man shriek in mortal agony. He wheeled about, and something in him that had been fighting hot, froze in fear.

Sprawled on his back on a counter, one outflung hand still twitching at a cereal box, was the man who looked like Satan. They had caught up with him—and so had death. From the chin down, his face was being corroded away, and the dark little store was strong with the fumes of acid.

Nat heard Harry utter a tense, "My God!" but he couldn't say anything, himself. Fool! he told himself bitterly as into his mind crept the terrible knowledge that he'd fallen for a stall. The man who looked like Satan had been sent to decoy him here—when he should have gone to Kathi!

Somewhere in the darkness, fleeing from here, was the murderer of the man who looked like Satan—but even further away, there was the pale beautiful girl with terror in her eyes, the girl he had promised never to let down.

"Harry," he managed, "this is your job. It's murder—you're a cop. You stay here. I'm going back to the Concord."

"Yes," said Harry. The old man's eyes were baffled, uncertain. "You go back there, Nat! You'll be safe there."

Safe? If there were one place in town that was safe from the corpse-maker he was looking for, Nat knew it was the dark little store where he was leaving Harry. His prey might double on his tracks a thousand times, but he wouldn't show up here again.

HIS HEART was rapping out an angry tattoo when he got back to the Concord. If anything's happened to Kathi....

Why had he been fool enough to trust her so long with Lorimer? The man simply wasn't equal to the situation.

He heard voices, Lorimer's and a woman's. A woman who was not Kathi. She wore a tailored suit, and she had a black eye. She took a long squint at Nat, and then: "That's what I mean! Who is this blond interest in Kathi's life? Ed, you know I'm square. I won't print anything you don't want me to. But everybody has a right to know why Kathi's been nearly murdered twice tonight. Let me talk to her, Ed!"

Lorimer's hands were clenching and unclenching, and he kept swallowing. "She can't see anybody. I won't tell you a damned thing till tomorrow." He looked miserably at Nat Perry. "I thought you got lost for good," he whispered. "You brought this pestilence on us"—he pointed to Nellie Jackson—"and you'd better get rid of her."

The Jackson girl backed away. "All right. I'll go. But you don't have to blame anyone but yourself if I make up my own explanation of what happened!"

Lorimer groaned. "Give me five minutes alone with this guy, can't you?" he begged. "Just five minutes." He rushed him into the next room.

"Where's Kathi?" Nat demanded.

The acute unhappiness deepened on Lorimer's sharp face. "She's gone."

Nat knew that something kept him from sailing into the man, but what, he didn't know. He wanted to wreck him—and more than that, he hated himself. He'd fallen for a stall, he'd gone way off track, and in that time, Kathi had gone. "Kidnapped?" he heard himself ask.

"No." Lorimer seemed to be growing smaller, as he met Nat's blazing gaze. "She just went out for a minute, and she never came back. I'm afraid to go around asking—but I know she's gone." His voice rose, self-pityingly. "Do you think I was such a fool, locking her in right after they got Renée? Do you think I don't know… and what the hell am I going to tell this Jackson dame?"

Nat pressed his flat hand hard against his hip, to keep him from striking Lorimer with it. "I'll shut her up," he said. "You stay put. If you've been lying, you won't last long enough to apologize."

It wasn't shutting up that Nellie Jackson needed, Nat considered. It was loosening up. She was going to talk now, and talk plenty.

Nellie Jackson wasn't going to talk, not until Doomsday. Nat found her in the corridor just outside the suite, her body contorted, but still. Acid had burned her eyes away.

CHAPTER SIX

AN ACCIDENT FOR THE BLEEDER

NAT STEPPED back from the gruesome figure, half-blind himself from the sickeningly familiar fumes. A swift hideous vision of Kathi's beauty meeting the same fate steeled the hatred in him.

She had broken down. He had let her break down, Nat told himself a thousand times as he drove blindly to the Star Club. He should have thought of this before.

The Star Club was silent, dark, though it was not yet curfew time.

A solitary patrolman guarded the entrance. Nat recognized him. "Anyone been here, Reilly?" he asked.

Reilly shook his head.

No, no one would have passed Reilly. Nat nodded, ducked around to the side street. The delivery entrance was modest, almost undiscernible.

He tried the door, felt it yield to his push, the snap taut. It was held on a chain. He looked about, saw Reilly deliberately not looking his way. Reilly was giving him a free hand.

In his pocket, Nat found a thin supple steel spring that had proved a handy thing to carry before this. His dextrous well-trained fingers worked the slim spring into the wedge of the chain, until the last link moved as he pulled. Gently he coaxed it toward him until the heavy end of the chain fell.

Nat slipped into the dark interior, feeling for his gun. Delivery cellar, pantry, kitchen.... At the swinging door between the kitchen and the main dining room, he paused.

Leather creaked behind him. He whirled about, his hands moving swiftly in an instinctive gesture of defense. But not quickly enough to evade the thick dark fabric that fell smotheringly over his head and shoulders. He felt strong muscles pinning his arms to his sides, and in the dark, he was unable to direct his struggles.

There were two of them—maybe more. It's curtains for someone, Nat thought savagely.... God, he still didn't want to admit it was going to be himself!

They caught his wrists, trussed them crudely and quickly, and marched him through a corridor which was invisible to him. He was going to a damp place, a little-used place.

He heard a girl cry out, and a man laugh. Both sounds echoed, as though they were being uttered in the bowels of the earth. His captors pulled the fabric from his head, and he found himself in the gloom of the wine cellar of the Star Club. Standing in front of him was the narrow graceful figure of Ramon Cordoba, owner of the Star Club. It was he who had laughed.

A little behind him, a girl sat hunched in a big chair, her small body wincing. At the sight of Nat, she sobbed, half-rose.

Cordoba pushed her back with a wave of his arm. "You'll get your chance at him," he said, "but don't let's rush."

The men who had brought Nat in, two big-jawed uglies, chuckled hoarsely. They were still each a little to one side of him, against the wall. The musty smell of the place was beginning to suggest something other than wine to the blond detective.

"Don't I get the acid bath?" he asked Cordoba. "You haven't taken this much time about using it before."

"No, you don't get it," Cordoba answered. "Can you guess why?"

Nat knew. "Because there's a cop outside," he said. "You know he must have seen me come in—that I'll be looked for. And when I'm found, it'll look as though I had met with an accident. Is that it?"

"Exactly." Cordoba's thin, humorous mouth curled slightly. "In the dark, you will stumble against something—cut yourself. It's well-known that you're peculiarly vulnerable to accidents of this sort. I can't be held responsible for the scratches."

"You'll be held for plenty of other things," Nat told him. "Enough people know who Kathi was afraid of. Enough people will know you're Luke Carman, a convicted murderer...."

CORDOBA laughed. "An interesting point of law, that. No man can be put in jeopardy of his life twice for the same crime. What is hopefully called my debt to society was discharged on an April morning, two years ago."

"That? That's over with." Nat's brain was working clearly now. "You had your gang steal your body after the execution, on a long chance. You'd lost enough weight to gamble on your neck not being broken. They used oxygen or something like that to bring you to—a pretty poor use of oxygen, I think personally. Well, they can't hang you again—but you've done enough work tonight to send you to the chair in New York State."

"I doubt it," said the night club owner. "I seriously do. In the first place, my organization is also effective in shielding me even from suspicion. You saw what happened to one of its members who was clumsy enough to attract your attention.

"As for Mary, or Kathi, as you call her, I don't think she'll talk, either. She'll have too much at stake herself. It's she who will give you the cut that's going to look to the police like an accident. She knows that if she doesn't, she still has a sister in Nebraska who's not out of my reach."

That smell Nat had noticed when he was first brought into the cellar seemed to permeate the place. And it was too tart to be wine. His eyes fell on a row of bottles, on the opposite wall, ostensibly wine bottles, but.... A sudden conclusion leapt into Perry's mind.

Cordoba was offering a knife to Kathi. "I'm not asking you to kill him, my dear," he said sternly, as she cringed away from him. "Just a scratch; the tiniest little scratch. It's so little to do, to save your sister's life."

Something happened to Kathi then. His warning yell joined with the others', as she shrieked wordless defiance, snatched a bottle from the shelf over her head, and hurled it at Cordoba.

The night club owner ducked, and Nat hurled his own body out of the bottle's path as his two guards released him and fled. He felt himself slam forward, clumsily, on his face at the same moment a chill howl of pain echoed behind him. The bottle had broken, and one of the pair who had brought him in was catapulting in wild panic from corner to corner, his face hideously blistered by the spattered contents. The other guard dashed up the cellar steps and disappeared.

SPREADING fumes made a twilit hell out of the cellar. Nothing was visible. Fumes in his throat, his eyes, and the yells of the dying man in his ears. Something solid and sharp grazed Nat's palm. He had managed to fall almost directly upon the knife that Kathi had been given by Ramon Cordoba to kill him with!

Tense, desperate, knowing he had only a second's time, and death to pay if he fumbled, he edged the cords that held his wrists along the knife's sharp single tooth. Surely, without wavering, he caressed the knife into an arc at the end of which was the cord. It sliced through. He was free!

The fumes had cleared enough for him to perceive dim shapes across the room. He saw Kathi struggling furiously with Cordoba. He was afraid to use the knife, in a melee like that—afraid he might lose even if he won. He sailed into them, aiming straight for Cordoba; caught the man's elbow, swung him around, from the girl.

Cordoba tried to straight-arm him, but Nat's fingers closed on the man's wrist, jerked it upward. In the same moment, he aimed the flat side of his hand mercilessly toward Cordoba's temple. It was a knock-out blow... but before Cordoba dropped, he crashed full-length into the shelf of bottles on the far wall.

Nat knew what was coming—or rather, his nerves and muscles did. He had to act too quickly for conscious thought. Even as Cordoba crashed into the shelf, Nat had pulled Kathi toward the comparative safety of the half-open door.

Behind them, there was not even a cry. Death must have come to Cordoba too swiftly for that. There was only a rising gas, so strong that it almost choked them before they reached the clean outside air again....

Kathi was swaying a little. As Nat hustled her toward his car, Reilly came up to them anxiously.

"Good Lord, Mr. Perry, you look—"

"Don't say it," Nat told him. "If you can dig up a gas mask, go inside. You'll find Ramon Cordoba in his wine cellar. I'd ask you to book him for murder, except that he's awfully dead."

Kathi echoed the last word. "Dead?" They were already driving toward the Concord. "But he can't die...."

"He's dead this time." Nat grinned. "Tell me—what made you go back?"

She shuddered. "There'd been so much death—I felt I could stop it."

"And you nearly ended by doing a little murder yourself."

Kathi's trembling little body was very close to him. "Don't!" she whispered fervently. "You mean that—with the knife? I couldn't have done that. Why, that was one of the reasons why I went back! He told me who you were: you're the detective they call the Bleeder. He bragged about how easy you'd be to kill when one knew your secret. I didn't know that when I called on you. If I'd known, I wouldn't have risked—"

Nat forced a laugh. "I wouldn't make much money, if all my clients felt that way. Forget it. Forget the whole thing. You're going away soon, you're going to be big-time. You'll be rich and happy, and you'll never think of this...."

Her voice was quiet, intense. "I'll think of you," she said. "I may even dream—troubled dreams. Why don't you give all this up? All this danger, this terrible exposure to death. Why don't you take what you could have so easily?"

For a second, Nat couldn't answer. She was so beautiful, he thought, and it might take so little for him to take that beauty to himself.... Suddenly he stiffened. "There's a man," he said. "An old man. I owe him everything. Even my life."

There was something in Kathi's eyes that Nat would never forget, and she said, "I think I know how that must feel."

FUNERALS—C.O.D.

IT HAD ALL THE
EARMARKS OF THE MOST
DESPICABLE RACKET
EVER DEVISED BY MAN...
OR MONSTER. AND NAT
PERRY, VERY VULNERABLE
DETECTIVE KNOWN TO
THE UNDERWORLD AS
"THE BLEEDER," WAS IN A
FAIR WAY TO CRUSH IT—
IF HE COULD COMB THE
HEARSES OUT OF HIS
HAIR!

CHAPTER ONE

THE THIRD HEARSE

PLAINCLOTHES INSPECTOR Harry O'Connor walked out of the commissioner's office, fighting for control of that odd smarting in his eyes. Younger men nodded uncomfortably as he passed, as though it had not been their inclination to nod at all. The old detective returned no salutations. They could think as they pleased, and be damned to them.

Still, the commissioner had been thinking the same thing. Harry wondered why his superior hadn't been tougher. It was no secret that many a younger officer had been busted for exchanging favors with Aaron Bluff—which was exactly what Harry O'Connor had been doing! Bluff was the nightclub king of New York—until the cops closed his hot spot on a public nuisance charge, pending a checkup for something worse. But that didn't faze Bluff. He had "loaned" money in important directions. O'Connor smiled to himself.... It was a damned good thing the commissioner hadn't seen him with Bluff the other night—in the *hearse*....

He had been a long time in harness, Harry thought with sudden desperation, and every year the going was harder. Just a little more time, he prayed, time enough to finish the biggest double-cross in history. And then, if he had to, he'd go out like a man. The thought ran over and over in his mind, a bitter, secret thing. It had gone that way all through his interview with the commissioner, so that he had heard only the trend, and not the phrases, when he was spoken to. Wait, all of you, till you see my diary. Maybe, by that time, you'll be burning Aaron Bluff for the murder of a damned old fool who used to be a city detective. But you'll be burning him for plenty besides, and when you're through, I'll be waiting for my innings at him in hell....

"Pop."

Startled, Harry looked up at the slender blond young man at the curb. He was a quiet-looking fellow, and his face was calm, but there was more trouble in his eyes than Harry liked to see. Was Nat against him, too? Nat Perry, the kid whose life he had snatched from Fate's maw, the kid he loved? He looked at a black coupe parked by the curb. "Buy a new car?" he asked lamely.

Perry shook his head. "No—smashed the other one up. I rented this till the green one gets repaired." His voice was gentle, concerned, as though he were talking to a child, and it made O'Connor furious. Hell, it wasn't Nat's place to care for him! Nat was twenty-nine, a

grown man, one of the shrewdest detectives in New York—but to Harry, he had been a son; and he was still a kid. "Pop, I want to know something: how did I happen to see you with Aaron Bluff last night?"

O'Connor snapped, "Probably because you snoop too damned much." Perry swallowed, and frowned a little, as though he couldn't believe it. He'd have to take it that way, O'Connor thought, and a sudden panic made him want to tell the young man the truth. Once he'd been Nat Perry's hero, and he had been prouder of that than of anything in the world.

He had reason for that pride. He'd given Nat Perry everything, and his first gift had been life, itself. There'd been no hope for that fourteen-year-old they found in the wake of a hit-and-run driver until Patrolman O'Connor gave him four blood transfusions, and imbued him with a fighting will to live. Only a broken leg; but Nat Perry was dying of broken skin. He was a born haemophiliac; his blood could not clot, and never would.

Wing somersaulted over him, landing
on his head beyond the desk.

AND NOW that fourteen-year-old was a man; a smoother-spoken, quieter man than O'Connor had ever been, and it was O'Connor who had reared him. A man who stood insistently before him, with faint damnation in his puzzled face.

"But, Pop, why pick a hearse for a conference? It's a good place for privacy, but what's private between you and Bluff?"

Harry shut his eyes, and opened them again. It wouldn't have been Nat's way of getting at Bluff, he thought—it wouldn't have to be. The Bleeder, they called Nat in the underworld. And they were afraid of him. No one was particularly afraid of Harry O'Connor any more.

Sixty's not so old, he told himself, but he didn't believe it, not when he looked at Nat. He should have quit—but he couldn't quit! Not with the terrible knowledge inside him that every case he'd touched for the past five years had been successfully closed only because the Bleeder was tacitly and inescapably behind him. He had to prove, even to himself, that he hadn't borrowed too much time from eternity… that he was still useful.

Best for Nat if I go, O'Connor thought. I got him into this kind of work in the first place. Without meaning to, or wanting to, I'm keeping him in it. He is the Bleeder, and his name was a name to reckon by, and always before, he had been too clever and too careful to die. But some day, if he stayed in it long enough, he'd hit the short end of the law of averages, and there'd be a broken old man mourning Nat Perry's sharp young wits and quiet young courage. Better if I go first, O'Connor thought….

What was wrong with the boy? Why must he still be staring with that odd heart-broken look on his face, and the spring sunlight full on his bared yellow hair? I'm a city detective—O'Connor told himself, as he retreated into the shadow of the white building—I have a right to my own ways without explaining them to a whipper-snapper of a private dick. He said, "What's wrong with Aaron Bluff? He's done me plenty of good, and I mean good." The words seemed queer to be coming from his own throat, but so many things about himself puzzled him now that he was old. "Beat it, you. And keep your face clean."

Nat Perry got into the black coupe, and drove away. That's what I've done with my life, O'Connor thought, watching the black coupe, and a certain pride came into him, so that his back stiffened and his eyes grew clearer.

NATHANIEL PERRY knew, two blocks before he reached Bluff's offices at Forty-second and Lexington, that he wasn't going to enjoy the interview. Aaron Bluff wasn't the kind of man he liked to deal with. They had never pinned anything on him big enough to fight—at least, not big enough for Nat to fight. The Bleeder knew his own vulnerability, and he disliked risking his life merely to prove how mean a man could be.

At Fortieth Street, he saw a sombre black vehicle in his rear vision mirror. The sight reminded him anew of last night. What had Harry O'Connor to do with Bluff—in a hearse? The answer must have been obvious to the commissioner, but Nat Perry wasn't the commissioner. Bluff had a payroll, and O'Connor must be on it. But Nat had known O'Connor too long to accept a thing like that.

Suddenly, the puzzle went crazy in his head. He couldn't think of it clearly, because just now he couldn't think of anything clearly. He always drove with his windows closed, which was one more item in his necessarily careful system of life. But clear warm air had been seeping into his coupe a minute before. Now, the warmth was abruptly gone. He was chilled to the bone and the breath left his lungs like air from a split balloon.

Death! He had been close enough to it before to recognize it. But now, there was no reason to die! He shouted, yet could not hear his own voice. It was like a dream, from which he was trying to wake. A shape moved past him, out in the sun-streaked avenue, and he knew it was the hearse he had seen in his rear vision mirror.

A hearse—for him? In a last defiant gesture against mortality, he tried to level his automatic toward the evil faces peering from the driver's seat of the hearse. But he had no strength. His gun arm slacked, the pistol clanking against the window.

Something roared thunderously in his ears, and a rush of wind made his crazily-pumping heart do dizzier tricks. For a second, he saw nothing at all.

When his brain cleared, he found himself slumped over the wheel, the automatic clutched weakly in his hand. His front bumper was kissing a traffic stanchion, and someone was bellowing from another car that he didn't own the road. A triangle of glass was missing from the front corner of his left window, and, three blocks north, a hearse was losing itself into traffic.

That hearse.... Some unreasoned clarity of purpose formed in his numb awareness, and his hand darted toward the gear shift. He had some idea of checking on the interest that driver had shown in him, but suddenly his body stiffened, and he leaned backward. He had been about to lean against something bright and gleaming that lay in his lap—it was the glass triangle, broken out of his window.

That, too, meant death. Something about that piece of glass brought Perry's thinking back to focus. He still felt cold, and more than a little shaky, yet he knew with lucid certainty that he had stepped into something. What, he didn't know. Probably the same thing Harry was in. His heart shouldn't have kicked up like that—there was no reason for it. Whatever else was lacking in his blood, it was pumped by as sturdy a muscle as any man's.

He was still shaky, five minutes later, when he looked down a short corridor at the large plate glass door inscribed:

AARON BLUFF, INCORPORATED

Suddenly, the things he had meant to say to Bluff seemed ridiculous. He had business with the man—as vital business as he'd ever had with anyone—but it had ceased to be anything they could talk over.

It would be pointless now, to ask Bluff why he interviewed policemen in hearses. Pointless, because Nat had already been answered in a way. Not a nice way. He had met a hearse, on his way over, and he had come closer to death than he liked to. If Aaron Bluff had written him a letter about it, he could have been no more sure that Bluff had tried to kill him.

But he couldn't accuse the man of that. He couldn't accuse him of anything—yet. He kept watching that glass door. Aaron Bluff, Incorporated. Incorporated what? What was Bluff's business these days? Nat wracked his memory, and discovered the surprising fact that Bluff had no business, as far as he knew.

THE GLASS DOOR opened briefly, and a girl was coming down the corridor. There was grim concern in her face. Whatever Bluff conducted behind that door, she knew about it. She might be his secretary, on her way to lunch; a client, or even a girl friend—it didn't matter.

Nat touched her elbow. Before he could speak the girl jumped away from him like a startled mouse. Her fear waxed to something like panic in the space of seconds. She ran from him, called to an elevator operator to wait, and hurried into the car as though there were a mad dog behind her.

Now, more than ever, Nat wanted to talk to her. He took the next car down, caught sight of her in the lobby. She was slender, too well-dressed to be Bluff's secretary, and not pretty enough to be a girl friend—of his. She couldn't have been more than twenty, and Bluff's affairs seldom involved innocents. Then who was she?

She entered a black limousine parked at the curb. Nat was close enough to hear her tense instruction to the chauffeur. "Dr. Etterley. Dr. Carl Etterley. Hurry!" He was not close enough to stop her.

As the limousine nosed out into traffic, Nat's rented coupe ground to a start. A bus swung out in front of him. He cut around it and then straightened out, just behind the limousine again.

No voice sounded from the larger car, but a second's glimpse told Nat that the girl in the tonneau was screaming. She beat against the shatter-proof windows with frantic gloved fists, her mouth a scarlet oval of terror in a blanched face. That wasn't fear—it was torture!

He pulled alongside, remembering his own recent experience in a closed car, and shouted at the chauffeur. There was no response, and a second shout froze in Nat's throat. He had seen that chauffeur less than an hour before, driving a hearse!

The coupe's chromium nose veered leftward, forced the limousine to stop at the curb. Perry leaped clear. When he opened the door of the tonneau, he knew he was too late. The girl's body sagged in his arms when he tried to lift her out, and horror had frozen onto her cold face forever. There was a coldness inside that car that didn't belong in a closed car on the hottest Thursday in May.

Nat turned to the chauffeur—but the chauffeur wasn't there. Everything had happened so quickly, so quietly, that an idle crowd was just beginning to gather around the limousine.

Through a clearing in the crowd, he saw a hearse rounding the corner.

The sight made him get back to his own car, quickly. Others would tend to the dead girl—any help he might have given her was useless now, and he couldn't even identify her. He pulled away, turned into the side-street, but the hearse was gone.

He was almost unnerved. Aaron Bluff—and three hearses. Maybe the same hearse, seen three times. Why had the girl died, as he had been intended to die? And what was her business with Bluff? What had been Harry's business with Bluff last night in that sombre death-cart?

It occurred to Nat that Bluff shouldn't have expected a visit from Nat Perry. There was only one man who could have told him of the possibility of such a thing. And that was Harry O'Connor.

There was an answer to everything, and he had the peculiar feeling that it was all contained in a little jagged triangle of glass which had come from his car window. There had been something about it, something more significant than just a deadly object for a haemophiliac to have in his lap. He realized that. But he didn't know the answer.

CHAPTER TWO

THE CORPSE DIED TWICE

HE PARKED in the East Thirties, and consulted a grimy telephone directory in a grimier drug store. Dr. Carl Etterley had offices on Park Avenue, and he lived on East Eighty-ninth Street. At the office, a feminine voice told Nat that the doctor was at home. He didn't 'phone again—he couldn't get what he wanted over a wire.

He didn't know the girl's name, but her doctor would. And her doctor might know other things. Doctors usually do. Maybe Dr. Etterley knew why a girl of twenty, who looked as though she belonged in another world, apart from Bluff, had been worth somebody's while murdering.

Maybe he knew what a girl like that could possibly have to do with a man like Aaron Bluff.

She had been an expensive-looking girl, and she'd had an expensive doctor. The apartment house on East Eighty-ninth Street had a lobby that might have been a ballroom. The uniforms fitted the doormen, and there was indirect lighting in the elevator. Nat rang the bell of apartment 8-A! It sounded three lilting musical chimes. They were very pretty, but not pretty enough to down Nat's rising ire when he heard footsteps and received no answer.

He rang again. This time, he heard nothing but the chimes.

Something was wrong. A doctor, even the richest doctor, is on call twenty-four hours a day, and anyone who lives with him knows it. If there were footsteps, there should be an answer. Nat took a small wire spring from his pocket; with it his dextrous fingers could open anything short of the mint.

A woman in a silk dress walked through the corridor. She saw a tall well-dressed young man fumbling with what appeared to be a key. She smiled sympathetically, and walked on. Nat smiled back. When she rounded the corridor, the lock was open.

It was mid-afternoon, but the foyer was dark. So were the other rooms—green shades had been pulled against the afternoon's heat. It was very cool, cooler than mere shutting out of sunlight could have made even an airy apartment on that hot day. It was almost chilly. And there was no one at home.

That chill—he'd felt it twice before during the afternoon. Once in his own car, and once when he opened the door of a limousine. A tremor of anticipation rose in him as he drew the blinds in one room after another, looking for the person whose footsteps he'd heard outside. He found the studio portrait of a handsome woman of thirty on the grand piano in the living-room. "To Carl, all my love, Bea." And the frame was draped in black.

Here was death again, death softened, death that could be displayed on a grand piano. Apparently Dr. Carl Etterley had been recently widowed. Perry thought of that other display… three of death's vehicles, that had passed before him since his abortive visit to Aaron Bluff. He had a sudden mental image of Bluff as a distributor of fashionable death—it had to be that way. He stepped into the next room.

Stretched on a candlewick bedspread, there was a handsome stoutish man who looked sick in the sudden sunlight. His limbs were tensed, as though in secret pain, and the carefully shaven skin of his face was the color of a frozen pond. Over the left breast pocket of his dressing gown was the maroon monogram C.E., and the letters did not stir.

"Dr. Etterley!" But it would take more than a cry to wake Dr. Etterley. A shove would not do it, nor the touch of a warmer hand on his. There was only one loud trumpet to which Dr. Carl Etterley would respond again. The corpse was cold. A coroner would say that Dr. Etterley had been dead at least twelve hours, Nat guessed.

But he had touched another cold corpse that afternoon—a corpse which had been a living girl ten seconds earlier! Now his own hands were damp with sudden, chilly sweat as he bent over the doctor, his mind trying for some reasonable diagnosis for this sudden epidemic of corpses.

Cheerfully, liltingly, the musical doorbell of the apartment sounded through the dank, cold air.

THE MAN at the door looked surprised when he saw the blond detective. Anyone might have been surprised to meet that particularly intent look with no compromise in it, over an ordinary apartment threshold.

He was a polite little man, though, and he peered at Nat almost tenderly over his thick rimless spectacles. He said in a softened voice, "Dr. Etterley—may I start attending to him now?"

It wasn't loud, but it made the little man jump. Nat said, "Who the hell wants to know?" and he kept his fingers tight around the man's lapel when he said it.

"Dear me. I'll be *glad* to go away if you don't want me! We don't usually take these rush calls. We only hurried this time as a favor!"

There was something undeniably genuine about the man's half-fearful indignation, as though he honestly thought Nat a madman, and a boorish one. The detective's hand dropped to his side. "Wait a minute," he said. "I think there's a misunderstanding. Where do you come from, and who sent for you?"

The little man drew a white business card from his neat black suit, and leaned forward on tiptoe to point his name out to Nat. He was Asa Hammer, representing the Douglas James Funeral Parlor. "Someone phoned us this morning, and asked for a man to come for Dr. Etterley. It's all very queer. The doctor—he is dead, isn't he?"

"Yes," said Nat. "Excuse me." His voice was too quiet this time to startle the little undertaker—but he felt anything but quiet. He dashed back to Dr. Etterley's bedroom, which seemed to be the direction whence that faint sound had come… the sound a man stirring in sleep might make.

Whoever had stirred, it was not in sleep. In sleep, no one buries a knife in his own heart. For in the maroon monogram over the doctor's left breast pocket, there quivered the erect hilt of a knife. But the doctor had been dead! Someone had called an undertaker for him that morning! Did two people want him dead? There were three doors in Dr. Etterley's bedroom, with a bathroom beyond one of them. The bathroom was empty, and its other door was locked. Someone had escaped through it; that someone had knifed Dr. Etterley and gone into the adjoining bedroom—

Nat didn't find anyone in the other bedroom. He didn't go there. At the front door, where he had left Asa Hammer, a man shrieked once, and then was still.

The little undertaker was slumped across the threshold, his eyes astonished. There was a little black hole in his forehead.

NAT PERRY got nothing from the smartly-uniformed elevator operator. He had taken a lot of people down, the man stammered; he had seen nothing extraordinary, heard nothing, and didn't want to believe anything. Nothing like murder had ever happened in his neighborhood before. The doormen were equally co-operative.

It wasn't Nat's job to quiz them. The police could find out who had killed Asa Hammer and struck a knife through the corpse of Carl Etterley. Nat's business was with another man, a man who had tried to kill him and who had started him on a trail that was spotted with death.

Aaron Bluff—Nat was convinced he was the man. Behind Aaron Bluff, was the figure of his foster-father as he had seen it last night, stepping out of a hearse. He was going to Bluff's office again, and this time he knew better what he had to say to the man. Few words would be exchanged, but they would be to the point, and followed by action.

There was no light behind that anonymous elaborate plate glass door on the fortieth floor of the skyscraper. The door itself was locked. Nat laughed dismally. He had found out one thing about Aaron Bluff's business, at any rate—shop was closed before six. He could find out more. Once again the Bleeder picked a lock.

He found himself in an airy waiting room, overlooking the East River. Bluff couldn't be doing badly, he thought. A door marked Private beckoned him further.

Aaron Bluff had salvaged at least his office furniture from the debacle of his nightclub. There was a box of cigars in the top drawer of Bluff's desk and a flat fifty of fancy cigarettes, the kind that women put in long holders and men don't like to be caught with. In the bottom drawer, there was a pinch bottle of Scotch and a quarter-inch thick cardboard folder.

Nothing else in the office, anywhere, suggested that Bluff was a business-man. The waiting-room was upholstered, innocent even of pencils—and except for a fountain pen stand and an empty filing cabinet, the office might have been a sitting-room in a private home.

And in the cardboard folder, there were exactly two receipts, in carbon. One was dated late in February, stating that Aaron Bluff had received two hundred dollars from Henry Burnside. The other, dated last month, acknowledged the same amount from Mrs. Beatrice Etterley.

Things flashed rapidly through Nat's mind. "To Carl, all my love, Bea." A photo—draped in black. Mrs. Beatrice Etterley had known the nature of Aaron Bluff's business, and she was dead, and her husband was dead. A girl had come out of Bluff's office to die within minutes. What kind of business was it, that contact with it was so fatal? What kind of business could keep Bluff going, on a visible intake of four hundred dollars in three months, when four hundred dollars obviously wasn't enough to pay the office rent?

Nat wheeled sharply as he felt the sudden draught. The door behind him was open, and the man on the threshold had his finger on the trigger of an automatic.

PERRY whirled sideways, letting the bullet sing into the desk's mahogany side. He recognized in the short nattily-dressed gunman one Ownie Wing, a bookie who collected in blood if he couldn't collect in coin. Wing had good reason to protect Bluff's secrets. When Bluff went down, Wing would go down with him. It was self-protection, and Wing was taking it seriously.

Nat took the same idea just as seriously. He dove at the bookie's ankles, a measured cadence of bullets rapping out over his head. Wing sprawled forward, over the detective's tense body, and the gun skidded a few inches on the carpet. Nat came to his feet, gracefully as a cat and Wing somersaulted over him, landing on his head beyond the desk. This was Nat's fighting style, this studied co-ordination of every muscle in his body. It wasn't new—it had been used in the East, centuries earlier. Scientific, requiring a minimum of effort in the application, based on exact knowledge of his own and his opponent's anatomy, the technique was a deadly weapon for any man who took the pains to learn it. It was this technique which had made the Bleeder feared in the underworld—it was complemented by simple-looking blows which had killed men Perry dared not leave alive behind him.

Wing moaned. His head was twisted queerly to one side, but he managed to raise himself, holding onto the edge of the desk. He looked at Nat, and in the falling dusk of the curtained room, seemed to realize for the first time whom he had attacked. "Bleeder!" He started to talk, hectically, in a high-pitched voice that had the hysteria of pain running through it. "My God, Bleeder... you're making a hell of a mistake! I didn't expect you here... your old man...." He paused, and his breath came heavy. He looked at Nat with his little eye's like a trapped weasel's.

"Shut up about my old man," Nat commanded.

"Like hell I will! This cinches it. Tomorrow anybody who reads the papers is going to know it. Your old man's a wise guy, Bleeder—but he can't play two ways with us! And you don't dare touch me for it, because you know—"

Nat's arm reached out, described a short vicious arc that ended at the side of Wing's throat. The man gasped. His face turned purple, and he crumpled backward like a stack of paper. "You won't talk about him," Nat said, "because your mouth isn't fit to say his name."

Ownie Wing did not answer. There was another reason for his not talking. He would be saying nothing at all from now on. Nat's blow had fractured his jugular.

The detective's hand shook a little as he pocketed those two receipts from the cardboard file, whether from anger or shock, he wasn't sure. He's had no compunctions about killing Wing—it was mere life insurance on his own part. But Harry—Nat had killed a man to keep Harry O'Connor clear. And he wasn't sure himself, that Harry O'Connor belonged in the clear.

He sighed. That wasn't his business. They'd quarreled, and maybe O'Connor had broken faith with his employer, the law. He hadn't quite broken faith with Nat Perry. There was that memory between them, that undeniable fact that the Bleeder had lived to walk the streets only because of O'Connor. There were other things, things that had happened in all the years of their intimacy.

Because of those things, Nat would have silenced any man who threatened what Wing had threatened... even a man who hadn't tried to kill him first.

It gave him a queer feeling of instability, to be working on the wrong side of the cloth from Harry. He had a pictured image of the old man before him now, a sawed-off, broad-shouldered old man with tired blue eyes and a gait slower than had been the gait of that man who gave him new life fifteen years ago. It was a long time since he'd taken advice from Harry, or needed it—it was a long time ago that Harry started needing him. Maybe Harry still needed him. He had to think so, anyway. He had to think so, if he wanted to keep going.

Maybe I needed him too, Nat thought. Maybe I always will. He knew where he had to go next, and he knew he had to get there in a hurry, because a man's life depended on it—but somehow, the life of that stranger seemed less important than it would have been if Harry had cared about it, too.

He forced himself to think of the urgency of this trip as he drove southward. Henry Burnside had transacted business with Bluff. It had not been the kind that Ownie Wing transacted with him. Hal Burnside was captain of the undefeated Overbrook Polo Team, and the papers had given him a build-up as one of the hardest-training, cleanest-living athletes in amateur sport. Therefore, Hal Burnside bade fair to be transferred shortly from the sports page to the obituaries.

When he stepped out of the elevator on the fifth floor of the house on Washington Square, Nat suddenly stopped forcing himself to think about the puzzle of Hal Burnside and Aaron Bluff. He didn't have to force it—it hit him between the eyes. There was a man standing at the door of the Burnside apartment, explaining to someone on the other side that he had to get in.

The man at the door was Harry O'Connor.

CHAPTER THREE

THE BLEEDER'S DESTINATION

NAT COULDN'T see the man on the other side of the door, but he heard the voice clearly. It was a cool annoyed voice, and it sounded as though its owner were recovering from a slight touch of amusement. "Of course you're a policeman, Inspector," he said. "I've already taken your word for it. But we don't want the police. I take it you're supposed to be a public servant—not a public nuisance. So will you please leave us alone?"

Harry O'Connor's face got the look on it that Nat remembered from crises past. The old plainclothesman started forward. The door slammed in his face, and the lock snapped with a sharp, cutting click.

He stood there for a moment, glowering at the door, as though he were of two minds about breaking in.

Then the look faded, leaving nothing but a bitterness that had become almost habitual of late. If Nat had ever seen a man angry, that man was his foster-father. There was a good reason for Harry's wanting to get into that apartment; there was generally a good reason for anything Harry wanted to do badly enough. But it apparently hadn't been good enough for a search warrant!

The old man's eyes met Nat's face, and the ghost of surprise crossed his lined face. His voice had no warmth. "Looking for me?"

"No, Pop, I—" Nat stopped. That wasn't true. He had been looking for O'Connor, all day. He knew that, by the feeling it gave him to listen even to O'Connor's surliness. He felt less alone, and completely confident once more. He didn't know Harry's game. He knew why he was here himself, but he didn't know what had brought Harry here. Even if it were the same thing—he didn't like to think of how Harry had found out. Bluff might have told him, last night in the hearse....

But those questions in his mind—were only questions. The important thing was that O'Connor was here, and whatever trail he'd followed could wait till later.

They stood there for a moment, the young man and the old one, and the old man's bitterness seemed to cover a certain shame. Nat wanted to tell him it didn't matter about that quarrel, but he couldn't—they hadn't quarreled that way before, and consequently, they had no experience in patching up after.

In the next moment, they weren't looking at each other, nor were they standing still. From inside the Burnside apartment, a woman's voice, forgetting all reticence in pain, shrieked, "Oh God, *help* me!"

They didn't have to do anything about the locked door. It opened of itself before them, and a man whose full fair face was twisted and ashen shouted at them, "Inspector—it's my wife! For God's sake, get a doctor!"

The two men rushed past him, into a bedroom where a woman lay taut and still, as though she had stopped moving in the middle of a convulsion. She was stretched across a chaise lounge, her long white fingers biting into the upholstery, her blue dress clinging to her body moistly. When Harry touched her, his mouth went tight, and he showed Nat his hand. It was wet. Nat understood that. There was a cold dampness coming out on his own skin... it was something in the very air of the room. They turned her over. The pretty face—it must have been pretty, before it turned almost the same dark blue as her dress—stared at them in numb, perpetual horror.

Hal Burnside stood at the threshold, his face quivering, his big hands rubbing aimlessly against one another. He looked helpless and a little awed. He said, the way a large child might have said in the face of disaster, "Aren't you going to call a doctor?"

With a practiced hand, Harry O'Connor touched the young woman's wrist, her temples, her heart. He looked at Burnside, and said in a flat, unhappy way, "Of course. I'll call our own medical examiner. But I can tell you all he could. She's dead."

"ISN'T this going to tip your hand, Pop?" Nat asked.

O'Connor's eyes were bright in the darkness. Too bright, Nat thought. "What the hell do you mean?"

"Even if the medical examiner calls it heart failure," the detective continued slowly, "would you let a hearse call for the lady, and take her away—for good?"

O'Connor didn't answer. He simply stared, numb. To Nat, it seemed almost natural... like the other holes he had helped the old man out of. The Bleeder began to feel on familiar territory again.

He'd been playing a close game with the murderer, O'Connor had, and now he had reached a showdown too early. Nat knew it. It was all Bluff's move now.... Bluff had sent O'Connor to see the Burnsides deliberately, because he knew what was going to happen. Harry had two ways of sinking deeper into the hole, and no clear way out. He could either aid and abet Bluff's scheme by keeping his mouth shut— or he could put his own hand on the table, a hand with no trumps in it. There was evidence, if he didn't let them bury the body. Not startling evidence. Just a young woman whom the police medical examiner would declare dead of heart failure. And heart failure isn't murder.

There was evidence somewhere, Nat thought, something he could pull out of his memory, something he could slip up the old man's sleeve himself and play for a jackpot. And then he had it. It was a little jagged triangle of glass, that had been broken out of his own windshield.

"Never mind, Pop," he said, "I'll take care of this end. You keep playing the way you started."

O'Connor looked at him, puzzled. Then he shook his head slowly, and left the room. Hal Burnside said flatly to the blond detective, "You don't belong here."

Nat looked again at the young woman who would shortly be pronounced dead of heart failure. "I know I don't," he said. He left.

He found a drug store across the side street from the house that fronted Washington Square. It was eight-thirty, a calm warm evening, and bare-headed girls strolled across the Square, humming as they went.

The Bleeder had a weapon now, one that Aaron Bluff had furnished himself. Nat remembered how oddly chill all those rooms had been for such a warm day. He remembered too, the knife in Dr. Etterley's heart. His fingers felt thick as he fumbled through the telephone directory. A name on a white card... and a polite little man, who had looked at him as though he were mad, and who had died shortly after.

Then he found it, the Douglas James Funeral Parlor. They had taken one call in a hurry; they would take another one faster than that.

"I'm sorry," said a man's voice, sounding not at all sorry, into the phone. "Too short notice—we couldn't manage."

"But you managed earlier," Nat stated, "when you sent Asa Hammer to Carl Etterley's." There was a short silence. "This may surprise you, but you're in line to have a neat series of murders pinned on you. You wouldn't like that, and neither would I—because someone else did it. You can call Inspector Harry O'Connor of the Headquarters for confirmation. Mention my name—Nathaniel Perry. Here's the address again... Washington Square South, Fifth floor. Burnside."

There was a pause, and then the voice commented softly, awedly, "We'll check. There'll be someone right over. Will they expect him?"

"Yes," Nat hazarded. He was sure that the first undertaker to arrive would be expected. "There's just one thing; don't *embalm* her. If you do, you'll run into trouble."

Someone exclaimed incredulously at the other end, and Nat replaced the receiver. He loitered just inside the drug store, unaware of the two girls at the counter who stared at him over their sodas, unaware of anything but that entrance on Washington Square.

The grey hearse, with the "Douglas James" on the left door in small script, pulled up in fifteen minutes. In an agony of apprehension, Nat watched the two men enter, waited for their return. If he could have thought for them, hurried for them.... But they had no inkling of the nature of this call, and Nat waited, his poised body giving no hint of the nervousness he felt. Suppose the others came before they left? Suppose Burnside—but Burnside wouldn't. Burnside wasn't staunch enough, at this point, to question details. He would accept whatever disposal offered itself.

The men came down. Between them they carried a box. Nat knew that Althea Burnside was in it. The medical examiner would pronounce no verdict over her, and the predatory hearses that had roamed the streets that day, like tumbrils looking for victims, would never hold her. Privately, Nat said a short prayer for the soul of Asa Hammer, who had been an honest man, sent on a murderer's mission to throw the Bleeder off the trail.

Slowly, the grey hearse lost itself in the shadows of Sixth Avenue. They were safe now—they had gotten away. They were good men, Nat thought in an ecstasy of relief, fine men. If he died tomorrow, he wanted the job of burying him given to the Douglas James Funeral Parlor, and he hoped they would make money on it. He could have pinned a medal on Mr. Douglas James.

And then he saw the second hearse streaming up to the door.

ONCE AGAIN, Nat Perry stood a little distance away from the door of the Burnside apartment, and saw someone refused entrance.

"But she's gone!" Hal Burnside was saying. "The undertaker has called for her!"

One of the three liveried callers laughed. It wasn't a friendly laugh. "All right, mug," he said. "This is a paid delivery. You asked for it—now you're going to take it." He nodded at the other two, and Nat saw his face. He had seen that face twice before since noon—once while he was trapped in an airless coupe, and once when he tried to stop the chauffeur of a limousine that carried a dying girl.

Burnside was yelping. His big stocky body blocked the doorway, and his face, that had been white when his wife died, was florid and ugly. "Take your damned foot out of that door—this house is mine!"

The liveried driver swung his arm back. There was something round and black in his hand, and it was set for damage. The man swung the blackjack through the crack in the door, which suddenly burst open. The two figures rushed inside, just as Nat started to run, and then the door slammed shut again.

He threw himself against the door, felt something heavy smashing into it from the other side. He tried the knob, and when he looked at the lock, he knew that it had been smashed. There wasn't a key in the world that could unscrew that mangled metal. Inside the apartment, he heard Burnside's muffled, "Don't! Oh God, don't do that! Please...." And then there was a crashing sound, as though someone were throwing furniture.

Nat heard his own voice joining the frightened chorus that echoed down the corridor, as one door after another popped open on the fifth floor. "It's a murder!" he shouted at them. "Call the police!" Someone, a very old woman, was tugging at his coat, begging him hysterically to take care of her, and he pulled away, and hurled himself again and again at the unyielding door.

Then, loud as sound itself, he heard an ominous silence from inside—and it drowned out all the other voices, and everything that was echoing frantically in his own brain.

For a second, he stood quite still, damning himself for a fool—the service entrance! Of course, they'd have used that! The silence inside the apartment couldn't have been more than a second's duration when Nat Perry darted past the corridor of excited tenants, through the one door on the floor without an apartment number on it. He was in the service hall, all right, and that grey door on his left had been left ajar—but he knew by the descending spot of light through the crack in the elevator shaft that he was just that second too late.

He took the staircase, flying down with his finger-tips barely steadying him at the bannisters. He reached the street just in time to see a black hearse disappearing at the far end of Washington Square.

Wherever they were taking Hal Burnside—or what was left of him now—was the Bleeder's destination.

CHAPTER FOUR

SPECIAL FUNERAL SERVICE

THE ROUTE was direct. He knew they hadn't suspected pursuit. His hands were steady on the wheel, and his eyes clear, but something was trumpeting in his brain almost dazingly. O'Connor—he'd get O'Connor in the clear once more.

Seventh Avenue South, merging at last with the unpopulated shadows of Varick Street.... Broadway at its narrowest, and east on

Canal Street. Then, south again… and east…. Once, at an intersection, a private car gave the hearse right of way after the light changed, but Nat picked the trail again at the entrance to the Brooklyn Bridge.

He followed at a discreet distance, merged in the traffic of Brooklyn's Atlantic Avenue, and then the hearse swerved into a crooked cobblestone side-street that ended alongside an elevated line. For two blocks, he followed under the El, the sound of his wheels and the hearse motor in front of him sounding loudly through the dark. Unless they were deaf, he thought uneasily, they knew they were not alone— unless they were less bright than he expected, they could have guessed who was following them.

He'd given them too much credit, he decided, when the hearse pulled to a stop in front of a pale and dingy storefront, unlit, inscribed, "Daniel Ferris, Mortician." They'd given him the show. He stopped, and peered at the street sign on the corner, to find the address. His pencil had made one thin line on a piece of paper when something jolted thunderously into the rear of his car. His hands flew instinctively ahead of him, and he tried to brace himself against injury to his face.

When he looked to one side, it was too late. The long lean face of the chauffeur of the hearse was faintly visible beyond an outstretched arm, and the sick sweetness of anaesthetic was making a blur even of that….

He felt sick before he opened his eyes, and sicker when he opened them. Alter a while, the dizziness and the sickness passed. He tried to move, and found it impossible. There was a pale overhead light glowing above in the ceiling, and within a few yards of him, there were men talking in low tones. He tried to see them, and couldn't. To either side of him, inches away from his face, were satin surfaces.

Then he knew where he was. He was lying, bound hand and foot, in an undertaker's parlor, flat on his back in a coffin.

He pulled at his arms, but they were stiff against his sides. Stiff— the word was unpleasant. One of the voices in the corner was raised to an audible murmur. "Hey, he's awake."

By the dim overhead light, Nat saw a handsomely preserved man of fifty bending over him. It was Aaron Bluff. He said, "Why, hello, Bleeder."

"Go to hell," Nat told him. His voice sounded faint, a little fuzzy.

"That's where you're going, Bleeder. When you spring the lock on the devil's private office, give him my regards."

Well, it was evidence he'd been after, Nat thought. He'd been sure Bluff was out for him—and he'd gone snooping for evidence so that Harry O'Connor could legally put an end to Aaron Bluff. And now he had his evidence. But it didn't look as though he were going to use it.

"It was nice of you, using chloroform," he said. "A knife seems to suit you better."

BLUFF made a deprecating gesture. "You'd have made a messy corpse that way. Besides, everybody knows you're too careful to tangle up with knives. No, Bleeder, you're going to be buried on the up and up, and not even that doddering old Pop of yours is going to have a come-back. They'll be mighty surprised when the Bleeder finally dies of heart failure!"

"You mean," Nat queried quietly, though the words echoed crazily back and forth in his own brain, "you're going to bury me alive?"

For a moment, Bluff looked startled. Then he said, "Let's not call it that. For all medical purposes, you'll be dead. And really, before we bury people, we're conscientious enough to embalm them."

"You're no undertaker," Nat went on. What was he doing? Stalling for time? That was hopeless. There wasn't a chance that anyone would trace him to this godforsaken corner of Brooklyn before that chill dampness he had felt so many times during the day became more acute, and finally permanent. "You're a salesman. You sell air-conditioning apparatus for homes and private cars."

"So what?" said Bluff.

"Listen," Nat told Bluff. "You are obvious to me—you'll be obvious to someone else, too. You won't drop the game, either—you're too pressed for cash. That's why you had to have the girl killed, this afternoon. You were so eager for business, you had to solicit it. I don't know who she was, but I'll take even money she had a rich relative, and was right in line. You offered to get rid of the relative, for a cut of the inheritance of course. She was a nice girl—she left you like she'd have left a cobra. She wasn't going to the police—not right away. She was just going to check with someone you'd given as reference— a satisfied client who'd been saddled with a wife he didn't want, and who had conveniently become a widower, Dr. Carl Etterley."

Nat paused, and Bluff remarked contemplatively, "Bleeder, how do you do it? I suppose you know you weren't supposed to get far enough to see Miss Turner in the first place. And now you turn up with her family history."

"It was a little piece of glass," Nat said. "I found it in my lap after I smashed my windshield. That's a funny thing, Bluff—for a piece of glass to fall in when you bust it. Something must have been pressing harder than I—say, at fifteen pounds per square inch. That something was air. And there wasn't any in the coupe. You had one of your men install one of your air conditioners in the car I rented, which could empty the space of air in less than a minute's time. Finally, I remembered how creating a vacuum lowers the temperature. You had another one of your gadgets in the girl's car. A thing like that must take quite a while to install and you couldn't have installed it while her car was parked outside."

Bluff turned up his palms. "As you say, I am guilty of creating a vacuum. Several vacuums. In other words, several nothings. And I'm going to show you the inside of one of them. That's what I'm doing to you—nothing."

"So I see," Nat remarked drily. "But you did more than that to Dr. Etterley, when your stooge and hearse-driver, Daniel Ferris, reported that I was about to call on the doctor. You were afraid I knew too much—that I'd work on Etterley, bring him to. He'd already paid to have that air-cooling apparatus installed in his home—you had killed him with it, or half-killed him, because being a normal man, he wasn't likely to keep mum about what was on his conscience. I got there too soon, so you had to use the crude way.

"It's a great set-up, Bluff. In the long run, you might even have charged the whole thing up to a technical accident. Your air-conditioners weren't even capable of killing people. You proved that on me. Your victims just went to sleep, and got embalmed before they woke up. But see where it gets you; somebody else is going to notice the same thing about a piece of glass. Soon you'll have to solicit more business, and the next customer may get further than the Turner girl did. And Harry—"

"Oh, Harry?" said Bluff. "I'm not bothering about him. I wouldn't waste the effort. I'll just let him break himself. He'll do a better job at it than I could."

Nat felt something snap in him at that. He surged upward, his body straining bitterly against the bonds that held it. Men were holding him down, and it was hopeless. He tried not to think about what was coming, as they closed the lid on the casket. Bluff brandished a screwdriver.... The cover shut down.

Then it came. The terrible cold, that ate into him like acid. The feeling of cotton stuffed into his lungs, the mad rhythm of his heart... and curtains....

SOMEONE said, "I think he'll be all right now, Inspector." For a second, Nat thought he was very young once more, and that he was getting over a traffic accident which had happened when he was fourteen. It felt the same way—and there was Harry O'Connor's face bending over him, with the marked disgust veiling an elegant pleasure, and he knew his head was in O'Connor's lap.

O'Connor said softly, "You make me sick."

Nat Perry touched his own face gingerly. It felt neither warm nor cold. That was probably because his hands and face were the same low temperature. But at least his hand moved. He flexed his knees, cautiously—they worked too. "Pop," he said, "how do I come to be alive?"

"Beats me," O'Connor admitted. "You were dead as hell when I found you." Nat looked to one side. There was a window, and dark streets were moving past the window. He was riding in an ambulance, he surmised, except that it was pretty fancy inside for an ambulance. "I'm getting pretty old," O'Connor went on, "to be running out to Brooklyn in the middle of the night to round you up. If you'd kept your nose clean, like I told you, I could have waited till morning."

"But, Pop—" Weakly, Nat tried to raise himself on one elbow, and realized that now he was going too far. "Pop, how did you know where to find me?"

"Couldn't have missed if I tried. There was a message for me when I got back from the Burnside place. It seems some dangerous lunatic called the Douglas James Funeral Parlor and asked them to pick up a corpse they weren't supposed to embalm. In this state, that was fishy. I took three guesses, and who did I suppose it was? Well, I was right. So I tailed you."

"Well," Nat protested, "at least I got you enough evidence to burn Bluff. Althea Burnside—"

"Althea Burnside doesn't remember what happened, except she

woke up scared stiff, with a lot of palms and lilies around her. Nobody's going to burn Bluff. He's dead."

"Heart failure?" Nat asked.

"Yah. Heart failure due to mayhem. He was trying to escape an officer."

Nat didn't ask which officer. He felt neither smart nor invulnerable, as he had grown to feel in the past eight years. He said fervently, "They're white people, the Douglas James Funeral Parlor. What did they call me again?"

"A lunatic," Harry repeated. "Old Doug was so excited he drove me out here himself. He's up front now. Want to thank him?"

Nat looked again around the interior of the ambulance—no, it wasn't an ambulance. It was something *else*. "No, Pop," he said a little feebly. "Just wake me up when we get out. I don't want to ride in a hearse again… for a long time!"

THEY DIE ON SCHEDULE!

NAT PERRY, THE INIMITABLE MANHUNTER CALLED "THE BLEEDER," LOSES A FIVE-THOUSAND-DOLLAR RETAINER, BUT WINS A BLOODY VICTORY OVER A CRIME MONARCH WHO KILLS AT WILL— BY NO VISIBLE MEANS! ANOTHER GRIPPING STORY OF THE WORLD'S MOST VULNERABLE DICK, WHO THIS TIME DOESN'T EVEN KNOW WHAT NEW FORCE HE MUST DEFEAT!

CHAPTER ONE

THE FROZEN-FACED BORGIA

IT **WAS** hot in the courtroom, but it was hotter outside. In the back, two attendants were laying bets on Virginia Wilder's chances of acquittal. Every one of the fifty-eight women who had managed to secure entry to the season's most sensational murder trial was taking mental notes on Mrs. Wilder's coiffure, and somewhere up front, a reporter was jotting down: "On the third day of her ordeal, the beautiful Borgia remained as impassive as on the first. This woman, against whom the state has built an airtight case for the murder of her husband, young Doctor Grant Wilder, sits beside her lawyer as calmly as though she were at a tea for the Ladies' Auxiliary of the Clinton Hospital...."

She was more looked-at than a visiting cinema star, more talked-of than Hitler. She had received enough fan mail, free advice, and crank threats to fill a cell the size of the one she occupied. There was only one thing about her on which all the world agreed: she must be smart; she could keep her mouth shut.

All the world, with one exception; a tall, blond young man in a suit of navy gabardine who was admitted to the courtroom after all others had been turned away.

She's a fool, Nathaniel Perry decided. Even if she's guilty, she's a fool. With a face like that, almost any alibi might have been meat for a lawyer like Arnold Ruppee.... He looked at the woman on trial. She was silent and grave and young, and before the curious transformation that comes over persons accused of grave crimes, she might have been beautiful. Beautiful in an almost professional way, and rather sweet. That, of course, didn't have to preclude murder.

Mrs. Wilder had given the press the worst possible impression. She had given her lawyer no impression at all, except that she seemed to trust him to defend her. Yet, two weeks ago, Ruppee had offered Perry five thousand dollars to unearth any data that might support a reasonable defense for his client.

Guilty? The police had virtually proven it, and she hadn't contradicted them. But Ruppee didn't take hopeless cases, and he had never lost a client, so far, to the chair. Ruppee must have seen some path to freedom for his client; five thousand is a lot to throw away on a futile gesture.

Nat Perry, through having worked with the police, respected their final opinions. His foster-father, plainclothes Inspector Harry

O'Connor of Homicide, had helped pile up incriminating evidence in the Wilder case. And now, as Nat leaned against the wall in that hot little chamber of justice, listening to testimony he had already heard, his thoughts drifted to the man who had brought him up. It would take a lot more than five thousand dollars to make him oppose Harry O'Connor.

O'CONNOR had saved Nat Perry's life at their first meeting, years ago. He had given an orphaned kid an example of nerve and stamina and morale that made him grow up into one of the shrewdest private detectives in New York. Harry was sixty now, not the man he'd been,

By all rights, that should have been the end of The Bleeder....

and sometimes he managed to get his work done only because Nathaniel Perry covered up for him unfailingly.

That was the debt of a lifetime, and the desire to pay it was Perry's reason for sticking to a career more perilous to him than to any man alive. His life was risked every time he took a case. The simplest violence might finish him—he was a haemophiliac. His blood was unable to congeal at even slight breaks in the skin. No, Nat Perry wasn't throwing his life away merely to substantiate the department's contention that Mrs. Wilder was guilty of murder.

Perry's wandering stare caught a return glance from Mrs. Wilder. She looked unseeingly at him, and then turned. The newspapers, because she'd given them no other peg for a soubriquet, had dubbed her the "Frozen-faced Borgia." But that frozen look made Nat Perry vaguely uneasy. It was definitely unpleasant to think of any woman going to the chair, especially as young a woman as Mrs. Wilder. He had already decided she was not too bright. It was barely possibly she could have another reason for her silence.

The more Nat thought of it, the worse he felt. Police investigation had hinted at no accomplice, but there mightn't be an accomplice. Besides, that was the only human explanation to someone who knew how silent she really was. Ruppee must have guessed at something like that.

He looked up expectantly as a new defense witness was called. The look of worry deepened on his face, and his hands clenched at his sides as he stared at the short, shabby Negro with defective teeth who answered to the call for Johnson Tolliver.

The man was sick, but it wasn't his sickness that brought an ominous silence into the packed courtroom. His wide white rolling eyes had an unseeing terror that made Perry think with startled intuition of death and that fear which is stronger than death. A fear so strong it forced a dying man to stalk into a courtroom to testify—as though he were the victim of Voodoo, come back from a century-old grave to tell a story he had been bewitched into telling.

No one ever heard what Johnson Tolliver was about to say. The little Negro's arm was raised solemnly over the Book, and his lips were parted to repeat an oath, when the invisible thunderbolt struck.

Suddenly, before a silent, shocked courtroom, the Negro's face went the color of grey ash, and his features screwed into a mask of pain. His left hand clutched his abdomen, but that solemn right arm, the arm he had raised to bear witness, stiffened in mid-air, rigid as in catalepsy.

A silent eternity was compressed into a second—and then the silence splintered as Ruppee's witness screamed wordlessly to the invisible power which had stricken him.

Before anyone had time to move toward the fallen man, another shriek echoed again and again through the courtroom, the shriek of a woman.

IT WAS the Frozen-faced Borgia, breaking her silence at last. Over the heads of the confused attendants, Perry could see her. She wasn't human—she was a fury. It was as though she knew what had died on the witness stand, as though she had seen all faith, all ideals, withered by a blow from nowhere, and known herself a helpless party to the destruction.

Ruppee was trying frantically to calm her. No one helped. They were no longer citizen-spectators, those people in the court—they were a terrified herd, stampeding away from a brutal miracle.

Perry shouldered his way toward the defense block. He felt that Ruppee needed him. His own mind was as terror-gripped, for the time being, as everyone else's, but some vestige of normalcy reminded him that black magic is impossible. Normalcy gripped him more completely, when he reached Arnold Ruppee.

"Do you see now?" the pudgy little lawyer yelled over the chaotic din. "Not you nor anyone else believed my client innocent. You all had her convicted and condemned before she ever came to trial!" He whirled like a dervish toward the bench, where Judge Ferris was rapping vainly for order. "Johnson Tolliver's testimony alone would have freed my client. I demand a postponement until this murder is investigated!" He turned toward Perry, and his voice dropped. "And in case the police bungle this investigation as they bungled the last, my offer to you still stands."

It was too violent, too unheard-of, Perry thought. Sharply, he realized that if he took the case now, he might be called on to solve a black miracle single-handed. He might face alone this grisly thunderbolt which had turned a roomful of people into terror-stricken beasts.... He wrenched away from Ruppee's grasp. He had to look at Johnson Tolliver. There'll be a reasonableness to it, he felt, an explanation; something a man can understand who's seen death in all its recognizable shapes.

The corpse was ugly. Even in death, the right arm was as incredibly stiff and disjointed as a log attached to a man. A phrase leapt into his head, the only phrase that tallied with that sight. Blasted by lightning. And that was no explanation at all.

The one man who could have saved Virginia Wilder from death, according to Ruppee.... Was she *fated* to die? His eyes followed her as she was led from the courtroom to her cell. Turning, he found Ruppee's anxious face close to his own.

He tried to keep his voice cool. "Nice show, Ruppee," he said. He succeeded better than he expected.

The defense lawyer's eyes grew horrified, and once more Perry found his arm gripped tightly. "Show? You mean I— Perry, you're crazy!"

Maybe that was true—Ruppee looked saner than any other man in the vicinity. There was a surprising strength in the pudgy lawyer's manicured fingers, and a surprising lack of emotional upset in the grey intellectual eyes that alone saved his face from grossness. He looked exactly what he was: an attorney who has met his first break in a desperate case, the first incident that might conceivably sway public opinion the other way regarding his client.

"You can't help but understand what this means, Mr. Perry," he continued, more calmly, almost triumphantly. "Virginia Wilder was framed, and we're trying the wrong party. I can get her an acquittal on what we have now. But I want more than that. I want justice. For the last time, will you help us?"

Nat suddenly wanted to say *yes*—but he knew he was feeling more than he was thinking, that he was still infected with a trace of that rabid mass hysteria which hung like a tangible substance over the courtroom.

"Wait until I'm satisfied that what Johnson Tolliver had to say was important," he said slowly, "and until I've spoken to Virginia Wilder. After that—maybe."

The anxiety faded from the lawyer's plump face, and Perry saw beneath it the profound relief of a harried man. "Come with me," he said. "I think we can see her immediately."

THE STATE'S CASE against her was strong and simple. She had sent for help at four in the morning, and when the police arrived they found her husband dead. The amount of strychnine in his stomach must have been administered four hours previous, or at midnight, to kill when it did—and there had been no one in the Wilder home but Dr. Wilder and his wife. How could a shabby Negro have broken that case?

She was small-boned, delicate, and the most striking thing about her wan, sweet face and her low, quiet voice was fatigue. As though some tremendous burden had fallen at last from her shoulders, Perry thought, and she was finally free to think how weary she was. She apologized to both men for having made a scene in the courtroom.

"It was a ghastly sight. You couldn't help it," Perry said.

She shook her head, and answered with quiet abruptness, "That wasn't it. You see, Grant died like that, exactly like that, on the morning of April tenth."

Ruppee sat down heavily, his mouth wide open, staring at Virginia Wilder in the thin light of the cell block. The Frozen-faced Borgia was breaking her silence. Now she looked neither frozen nor sinister. She looked haggard and troubled. "Until now, it hasn't seemed to matter," she went on. "Nothing seemed to matter after that night when Grant came home to die. I didn't realize then that an innocent man might die because I had stopped caring enough to tell what I knew."

Was it her silence that had killed Johnson Tolliver? Silence on what? "Did you know the witness?" Perry asked.

She nodded. "He was a cab driver who had the stand in front of our home. He drove Grant away that night, and brought him home again at half-past two in the morning. Grant—was very ill. He died soon after.... I don't know how Mr. Ruppee found out. It wasn't I who told him."

Ruppee had been right. Tolliver's testimony would have cleared Virginia Wilder. The State's whole case rested on the fact that Grant Wilder had been home alone with his wife the night he died!

Ruppee hopped to his feet, looking like a huge ground bird. "Virginia! Where was your husband that night?"

A deep flush came into her cheeks, spread slowly over her face and throat. Her voice grew very hushed. "I didn't tell you before, because I didn't think I could be convicted of something I hadn't done. I loved Grant too much—I was too proud—to desecrate his memory if I didn't have to. He was with Peggy Anderson, his nurse. I lost everything but that memory—long before he died. But if I'd known another innocent life would be taken, I'd have told."

Ruppee said, with a brusqueness that barely concealed a note of triumph, "You couldn't have saved Johnson Tolliver. I'd have had to call him as a witness in any event. The world, Mrs. Wilder," Ruppee grew oratorical, "does not accept any person's unsupported testimony without corroboration, not even the word of an innocent woman like yourself.... Mr. Perry, what are you going to do now?"

Perry said, "I'm taking a stab at that corroboration. Where does this Peggy Anderson live?"

CHAPTER TWO

DEATH'S PERFECT TIMING

NAT WENT out into the June sunshine with a sense of startlement greater than he usually felt at the beginning of a case. His own susceptibility had in times past rendered him utterly ruthless with the underworld. In spite of his handicap, he was expert at equalizing the risks between himself and his enemies, yet he felt now that all his old defenses were useless in this particular case. That morbid sense of superhuman intervention he had felt in the courtroom had not died with his excitement. It remained, and grew stronger.

He tried to put it out of his head as he nosed his green sedan steadily through morning traffic, but it couldn't be done. He could think of other things, but only with thought processes. There was something inexplicable about Johnson Tolliver's death, something no amount of cool reasoning could clear up. It was that desperate compulsion which had made the Negro drag himself into court to testify— and to die.

The timing of that death! What earthly agent could have stricken a man down at the last possible moment? Was it some dark unseen power that Johnson Tolliver had defied? And if Grant Wilder had died in the same manner, as his widow said he had, had his death been timed also?

Timed to involve his widow in a skein of murder-guilt?

It wasn't possible. Grant Wilder had died of strychnine poisoning, and no chemist can predict the efficacy of strychnine to the split-second.

He was still groping for a credible solution when he pulled up in front of a cream-and-red facade on Charles Street, in Greenwich Village. It was almost unbearably warm, with the sun reaching its zenith, but there was an instinctive premonitory chill inside Nat Perry. He looked about. There were few people in sight. A small Italian boy with scuffed shoes and enormous brown eyes asked solemnly, "Watch your car, mister?"

"Sure." He gave the boy a dollar. He didn't know what he expected, and that was the worst of it, because he knew he could expect something. "Don't stand too near it, and don't let anybody see you watching. If you see anyone trying to monkey around, run for the cops. Understand?" The boy nodded, wide-eyed, and Perry entered the flashy-fronted building.

A thin girl with a white face under pale flaxen hair answered his ring at the third floor rear apartment. She wore a blue silk bathrobe, and she plucked nervously at the folds of it with her left hand, as a dope addict might fidget. Traces of un-removed cosmetic outlined her sharp mouth, looking ghastly in the daylight that filtered through the hall.

"Yes," she said too quickly, "I'm Peggy Anderson." Then she looked at him with an odd combination of terror and pleading, as though she were trying to determine whether he were wolf or shepherd. There was youth under the nerves and the stale lipstick, youth gone haywire and terror-silly as only youth can go. She was twenty at the outside. She was nothing a man in his senses would have preferred to beautiful Virginia Wilder.

But something else about her struck Nat. She was helplessly desperate as a puppet revolting against a puppet-master. Her terror had an un-human quality that made him think of Johnson Tolliver.

Was she afraid of the same thing? Was it visible, was it behind that half-closed door? "I'm a friend of Mrs. Grant Wilder's," he said, as gently as possible. "I want to talk to you. She doesn't mean you any harm."

The gentleness wasn't enough. "No!" the girl exclaimed. "You can't come in—you don't belong here!" Her hand dropped the loose edges of her bathrobe, and darted toward the door. It was a clumsy gesture, with no strength in it, and with comparative minute effort, Perry shoved his way in.

It was a neat little room, with a college banner across the wall above a studio couch, and reprints of good etchings on either side of a maple bureau. There was no sun, but the room could have borne the scrutiny of sunlight. It looked not at all the kind of room where a drunken party-girl would have entertained a drunken philanderer.

He asked, "Was Grant Wilder here the night he died?"

The girl had looked jittery. Now she became utterly panic-stricken. Her voice rose, as though to convince some unseen audience, and she cried out, "He was, he was! And I'm not sorry! He loved me, see! He came here—"

She didn't finish, and Perry saw why she was using that clumsy left hand to hold her robe. A certain stillness came to her thin immature body, and she jerked like a marionette on strings. Her mouth opened, as though to emit a scream, but the scream was never uttered. One hand clenched at her waist, and she doubled up on it in ghastly pain—but the whole right arm hung like a length of stone from her paralyzed shoulder. She staggered toward him, her face writhing in torment. He caught her as she fell.

When Perry felt for her heart-beat, he found nothing. She was dead. Dead, with the same look of torture on her face that had been on the face of Johnson Tolliver. Dead, with the testimony Johnson Tolliver hadn't had time to utter stifled on her parted lips.

There was a phone in the hall, and in a voice that sounded cool enough to be someone else's, Perry heard himself summoning Homicide.

HARRY O'CONNOR'S eyes narrowed into hard blue slits. "If you were anyone else on God's earth," he said ponderously, "I'd say you were deliberately pulling something pretty bad. Do you think we're trying to convict Mrs. Wilder for the fun of it? I don't know what she told you, but she didn't tell it to us when we were willing to give her a break."

"She wouldn't do it because she couldn't have told a trained cop a thing that would hold. She waited for a sap like you to come along—"

"Pop!" O'Connor had come into a room where invisible death had taken another witness, and the sight only made the old man more furious.

"—a sap like you," the plainclothesman continued implacably, "who'd run riot for sentiment. But you're not the only sap. Ruppee got your client free on bail. A very high-powered bag of wind, Ruppee.

As for that business in the court, there isn't a trick Ruppee wouldn't pull."

Perry's face went as hard as his foster-father's. It had to. There was too much going on inside him. It wasn't what O'Connor thought—that was understandable. O'Connor hadn't heard Virginia Wilder's story. It was the way the man felt.

"Give it up," O'Connor said more softly. "Nat, this isn't your kind of game. You've got half the crooks in town scared stiff of you. They call you the Bleeder—and they don't call it out loud. But the man who roped you into this belongs to the other half. He'll want you either on his side, or—dead!"

"At least," Perry answered, "I'm giving Mrs. Wilder the benefit of the doubt until she's proven guilty. That happens to be the law, but maybe you don't remember the law."

The two men exchanged stares, not in enmity, but in fright. The fright showed on O'Connor's face, and not on Perry's—but Perry felt it. And he knew that O'Connor's fear was for the man some called the Bleeder. As he turned to go, he knew O'Connor had said one undeniably true thing: he wasn't fighting an ordinary crook. The Bleeder had established enough of a reputation for deadliness to guarantee him a modicum of immunity where he was known. But this was different.

This time, he didn't even know from what he needed to be immune. He didn't know who was checkmating him, and more important, he didn't know how it was being done.

What had frightened the Anderson girl? Justice? But she had protested passionately that Wilder was with her on that fatal night, and if she read the papers, she must have known that would put her right in Mrs. Wilder's spot, removed only by hours from trial for first degree murder. Would she have felt safer in a spot like that—than where she was?

Because she would have been safer—and he was almost sure she had been lying.

Not his game? Not by a long sight. It didn't look like any lone man's game. But what he hadn't bothered to tell O'Connor, what the other man knew already, what had brought the fear into O'Connor's eyes and into Perry's heart, was that he couldn't give up now. He was in it up to the neck. Peggy Anderson's death proved that the killer knew he was working for Virginia Wilder. If Johnson Tolliver had been timed to die, and Peggy Anderson, then it was within the realm of possibility that somewhere, someone was making a memento of the Bleeder's name on the second hand of an incomprehensible clock.

CHAPTER THREE

MRS. WILDER'S CORPSE-GUEST

THE STREET was still innocent of people, even of the boy he had engaged to watch his car. Perry's eyes scanned the pavements, and on the diagonal corner, located a small wide-eyed figure, frantically waving him back.

He retreated into the doorway, one hand feeling toward his gun. He didn't understand now, yet he knew there would be trouble. The kid, having assured himself that his temporary employer was standing still for the time being, darted down the block toward Seventh Avenue.

The next ten seconds went livid, as though illuminated with hellfire. It had barely penetrated Perry's mind that the child was running toward a strolling patrolman a block ahead, when something like a war broke out immediately to the west. A gun crashed, and the pavement erupted into little scars.

Five paces from where he had started, the small Italian child dropped suddenly and horribly. The shooting stopped, and then Perry knew why the child had waited for him to emerge before running for the police.

After that shocking reveille of gunfire, Charles Street woke from its noon siesta to a rocking blast of sound. For almost a minute, fragments of Perry's green sedan continued to drop into the gutter. There had been an explosive under the car—placed there by someone who had foreseen the exact second of Perry's exit.

There was a red haze in his brain, and the vague shape of a certain realization in it. His mind flashed back to the loud, almost shouted protest of the Anderson girl, just before she died, and in that remembered echo, a number of things became clearer.

Another figure took dark shape, far up the block, on the shaded side of Charles Street, emerging from a delivery entrance. A man with a gun. This was understandable language at last, Perry thought savagely. He leapt into the street, started after the killer. His automatic was poised when something about the fleeing figure forced a sharp hoarse cry back into his throat and kept him from firing.

The killer's right arm was swinging like a pendulum at his side, stiff, jointless.

At the corner of Charles and Bleeker Streets, Perry's hand reached out to grasp a paralyzed shoulder. The swift moment of reckless rage was dead in him. He was facing—not the puppet-master, but another of his puppets.

PEOPLE were coming down the street, outraged people who from their windows had seen the child killed. The thin elderly man, hollow-chested under his worn respectable suit, struggled feebly in Perry's grasp as he gaped at them. "You've got to let me go," he whispered. "I didn't—any jury would acquit me! But I'll die if I don't get back to him—"

There was a cold certainty inside Perry that the man was telling the truth. Once, this oldster might have belonged to the same order of beings as those people who approached him with hot hatred in their eyes. Once, he might have been subject to judgment by their laws. But that time was gone. He was the maimed projection of another will, outraging the earth he walked on. He had the stamp of terror in his ashen face, the same terror that had marked Johnson Tolliver and Peggy Anderson.

They were dead, but this man was alive. He was Perry's only link to justice in the case of Virginia Wilder.

The crowd was thickening, but the patrolman had arrived, his eyes round and shocked. He recognized Perry, nodded curtly, and then tried to stem the mob from the detective and his captive.

"Please, please!" the man whimpered. "He'll kill me if I don't report to him—he could kill me a thousand miles away. I didn't want to hurt you. I'm not the one...."

"Who is he?" Perry asked. "What has he done to your arm?"

"I don't know! I don't know how he did it—" the frightened voice broke off, and for a moment, Perry thought the man was going to die then and there.

In a voice he might have used to soothe a lunatic, Perry persisted, "Tell me where he is."

The answer was a whisper deathly as a last confessional. "I can't be sure. He can be in more than one place at a time. You might find him now with that woman they freed on bail, the Wilder woman."

Behind him, Perry heard a short, shocked laugh with no mirth in it. "A nut," said the patrolman.

Perry said, "Get this man to a prison hospital—I'll report there later." He rammed through the crowd, into a cruising taxi at the curb. He heard himself give an address on upper Riverside Drive, and an order to hurry, but there were other words in his brain, and thoughts coming so fast that the words for them were half-formed.

A child had been killed in broad daylight, by a man deathly ill, with no motive. Anyone would call it insanity.

At last the ghastly aura of events shrouding the Wilder case began to assume a pattern. Nat Perry knew he had crossed purposes with the perpetrator of a devilish and brilliant scheme, who had so far enjoyed the added benefit of luck. But luck like that couldn't hold out—it was maniac's luck.

He was no longer surprised at the thought that the man he wanted would be at Mrs. Wilder's. It seemed the most logical place for him to be. A certain detachedness came to Perry, so that he could relegate the blood and the pain he had seen to another part of his mind. Maniac's luck, against the man who refused to die. Nat couldn't afford to doubt the outcome. He had to think as clearly as though he were playing with wooden pawns instead of flesh-and-blood ones, and as though the stake were infinitely less important than life and death. Much later, he would remember what had happened, and in Nathaniel Perry's cheerless thoughts, the child who had died on the pavement would die a thousand times again. But not now.

Fifteen minutes later he stood at a sloped curb, with the Hudson sparkling behind him, staring at a barren-looking window with its shades drawn. It still sported a small undusted plaque reading Grant Wilder, M.D. Wilder had been dead two months. But the apartment wasn't empty now.

The shade slapped violently, only once. Wind hadn't caused that, nor were his eyes playing tricks. He was on the verge of an encounter with the power that reached out of nowhere to kill.

THE DOOR to the apartment on the first floor was locked. There was a length of steel wire in Perry's pocket, and the Bleeder's fingers were dextrous. But time was limited. Whatever had slapped that shade had been moving quickly, and this was an unfamiliar lock. He pried the ends of the curved wire into the keyhole, and let them tremble among the tumblers, delicately, surely. The second time he tried it, there was a dull click.

Very quietly, he shut the apartment door behind him. He was in a dark hall, musty-odored, as though nothing had breathed in it for weeks. The darkness concentrated into the solid hurtling mass of a human body, flying into him, and the impact knocked the revolver from his fingers. The attack was sooner than he had expected. He glimpsed a fair-skinned face, lean and pale as his own, angry and intent, as he braced himself.

A hundred thoughts wrote themselves on his brain during the next third of a second. No terror-stamp of slavery on that glimpsed face. This was the man, not one of his underlings. This might be a trap, this might be the end of the Bleeder, but—his thoughts ended abruptly as the brief combat itself, as the dim apartment re-echoed to a shrill and soulless shriek.

Perry broke away from his antagonist, ran through the darkness, down the long hall. Virginia Wilder had shrieked like that, that morning in court. By the pencil-line of light that came through a crack in the shade, he saw her. She was crouched in an overstuffed chair in the carpetless living-room, her mouth a frozen oval. She was unharmed. It took strength to shriek like that.

He wheeled about, expecting to face his recent opponent. There was no one. No one in the hall, no one in the living-room where Virginia Wilder had grown suddenly silent. Nathaniel Perry had been close enough to put a bullet into his quarry's heart—and the man was gone.

He looked at his client with a kind of numb fury. There was still terror in her face. And then he saw that they were not alone. He followed her glance across a threshold into another room, where another woman was seated on a couch.

The woman wore a hat and coat, wrapped surprisingly close for the heat. There was a thick, sick-sweet odor in the heavy air about her couch. She did not speak as Perry approached, nor turn her head, and when he touched her, she fell abruptly on her side.

She was dead. He knew, from the odor, and the swollen look of decay on her face, that she had been dead for many days. Even in the coat, even after all that time, he knew by the right arm of the corpse that he had found all that was left of another crippled puppet.

The detective sought for the shreds of detachment in his brain, and did rapid mental arithmetic. The police had closed the apartment a month ago, and this body must have been here for almost half that time. It was the link he needed—the proof that the murder-series which began with the death of Grant Wilder had not been interrupted, merely to resume today.

He heard Virginia Wilder's gasps lengthen into sobs. He did not speak to her as he crossed the room and picked a dust-covered telephone from a side-table. He kept his voice low and distinct; Harry O'Connor's voice at the other end was neither. It was high-pitched, as an old man's voice often grows in excitement. "Nat? We've got the report on Tolliver. Ever heard of jake-leg?"

"Not lately."

"You wouldn't have, lately. It went out of circulation a good fifteen years ago, before they even repealed prohibition It's a distilled ginger drink, a hell-brew that the old-time hi-jackers used to sell at eight dollars a quart. It crippled some people, blinded others, and killed or paralyzed about two thousand kids whose parents thought they needed something for a cold. That's what Johnson Tolliver had in his stomach. There was something else, too, but we won't know about that till the examiner's finished with the corpse. Where are you?"

"I'm uptown," Nat said, "with Mrs. Wilder and a corpse. It's not such a fresh corpse, but keep that under your hat. You can use it as a peg to re-arrest her. She's guilty as sin, but I'll need a little time to make it stick."

CHAPTER FOUR

"TWO PLACES AT ONCE...."

HE HEARD a startled gasp behind him as he replaced the phone. Virginia Wilder's face was no longer merely white—it was livid.

She clutched at the back of a chair, and her knuckles were pale with the effort. Her cheeks blazed and she was beautiful. Beautiful enough to make a man lie and cheat and murder... beautiful and evil as the first sin. "You're insane," she said.

"Maybe," he admitted. "I'll grant you that—until I've cleared up the details. Though I'll have a hard time proving what I've just said. Obviously, the corpse in this apartment met death while you were in jail, which would seem to exonerate you. But even so, I'm not as insane as the man who conceived this hellish scheme."

Triumph crossed her face, fleet, desperate triumph, with fear and guilt beneath it. "So you see—" she began.

"You probably banked on that," he went on. "You and the man you've been working with. You expected that if anyone did get wind of your scheme, it would seem fantastic beyond belief. But Johnson Tolliver's death in the courtroom served as well as his testimony would have to indicate a frame against you—which made that spectacular timing seem useless to whoever wanted him dead.

"Then it occurred to me that it couldn't matter, from the murderer's point of view, whether Tolliver testified or not. The important thing was for him to die, so that his death could add weight to your innocence and point at someone else's guilt. Exactly the same logic applies to Peggy Anderson's death, except that she lied, and she spoke louder than necessary. She wasn't the actress you are.

"She spoke loudly—and yet there were only the two of us in the apartment. If it was true your husband was out most of the night he died she had undoubtedly seen him. That was why she was drawn into the case and terrorized. Adding those two things together, I would say he had been in the house, probably in the apartment next door to hers. That's where I'm going to look for your accomplice—and while you're back in police custody, nobody's going to stop me from finding the man or woman you and your co-worker must have planned for a frame."

There was a fiery quality about her that he had not seen before. "*Can't* I stop you!" she cried. "I'll show you! You won't dare go through with this! I'll tell the police you're assaulting a decent man—"

"And suppose the police find your decent man has assaulted me—fatally? Then they'll have a certain murder case. There isn't a chance of that, of course. But you think there may be."

Her face went grey again; the fire had died to an ash. Still, she held herself erect, her hands tight on the chair back. "You don't know what you're saying," she whispered. "I could show you that. And I could show you a great deal about love...."

He laughed, a sharp ugly laugh, and her eyes went wild with fright. Like a small trapped animal, she turned and bolted for the door. He stepped into her path, caught her wrists in his strong hands. She went limp without struggle. He could feel her body pressed close against him. Her eyes were shut, and she did not move, but her heart was beating furiously. She was playing her last desperate card.

For a moment, he knew how it must have felt to risk everything for her. Then he pushed her away from him. "Sit down," he said, "and don't bother trying that again."

She knew it was hopeless. She could neither lie nor flirt her way past him. Her hands reached out like a cat's claws. "You filthy Judas!" she cried. "You—"

As he seized her shoulders and held her forcibly away from him, Nat Perry's heart was somersaulting at last. She may not have realized it in her fury, but her fingernails were far from being futile weapons; they were capable of killing him.

That was how O'Connor found them. Perry turned to the older man, who stared at him bewilderedly. "You can make her talk now, Pop. I'll see you later and explain."

A PATROLMAN was walking up and down in front of the cream-and-red facade on Charles Street. He looked hot and intent, and at the sight of Nathaniel Perry, surprised. "Coming back for more?" he asked. "The old man's ready to give you hell when he catches up to you."

"The old man's busy elsewhere," Perry said. He went into the dark hall again, up the three flights of stairs. Two apartments on that floor, and he had been in one of them already. The neat white plaque on the door of the other read *Dr. Ralph White*. He might have expected to find another doctor, he thought. The lock was easier than Virginia Wilder's.

He was in a short foyer opening into what seemed an office. A lean, pale man sat in a tall chair behind a big desk, and his cold blue eyes met Perry's stare unflinchingly. It was the man who'd escaped him, the man whom Virginia Wilder's scream had saved from justice in that dark little hall uptown. This time, there would be no scream, and no intervention. Perry kicked the door shut behind him, bolted the chain with his left hand. The gun felt stern and steady in his grasp.

Dr. White did not rise, nor flinch, nor blink. There was a revolver on the desk, and a welling dark circle of ooze on the side of his head. He was dead.

Perry's hands went hot and wet, and he sheathed his gun. It wasn't suicide. Dr. White's arms were clasped on the arms of his chair. He had not died by those hands. Murder had forestalled justice once more.

Behind him, a voice said quietly, "Don't move now, or you'll never move again."

Very slowly, his hands held visibly at some distance from his hips, Perry turned round. Then he thought he was either crazy, or in another world.

If the man behind the desk, with a hole in his head, was the man he had tangled with before—so was the man with the gun!

"I told you not to move," the newcomer repeated. His voice was not cool—it was harsh, sibilant. "If you'd come ten minutes later, you would never have known that the dead man was my brother. You would have had a perfectly satisfactory scapegoat, and the eminent Dr. Ralph White would have succeeded in death, as he did in life, in denying the existence of his criminal twin."

"It had to be like that," Perry said very quietly. "Of course.... Peggy Anderson, who lived next door, was obviously speaking for your ears when she raised her voice to talk to me. I'd have been here much earlier if your poor murderous dupe hadn't told me you were at Mrs. Wilder's.

"There's nothing miraculous about a man's being in two places at once, White. Any normal mind, under ordinary circumstances, would immediately leap to the explanation of twins. But those weren't normal circumstances. You took that old man's mind and visited the living fear of death on it. You persuaded him that only you could save him from the slow, sure effects of the poison you had given him. You made him a monster who would shoot down a child.

"You knew I would go to Mrs. Wilder's—and so did she. You both knew that I would meet your brother there, because she had sent for him. You even hoped I'd kill him."

White grinned. "Fine, Mr. Perry. That's all I wanted to know. If Peggy Anderson's words led you here, then I don't have to worry about anyone else arriving immediately. How much else have you guessed?"

PERRY said wryly, "Enough to tell you that there's an excellent reason why you oughtn't to shoot me on the spot. But I'll let you do the guessing on that for a while. As for Grant Wilder's murder: he found out that you knew his wife rather too well. Taking you for your brother, he came here that night two months ago and met you, posing as Dr. Ralph White. You poisoned him that night, and sent him home."

White's face was growing pale, but his voice was still steady. He kept the gun trained on Perry, and the defiance in his voice indicated some inner struggle about using it at once. "Yes, and the scheme's going to work! Virginia's been vindicated. The police are going to find a confession among my brother's effects. I've built a small fortune out of my private business, enough to support Virginia and me some place where we'll never be found. We've got more than Grant Wilder's insurance; we've got the insurance on all the people whose beneficiaries I obliged."

"I see," said Perry. "That accounts for the old man and the woman whose corpse I found in Grant Wilder's apartment. Posing as Dr. White, you administered slow poison to your chosen victims for a cut in the fortunes of their heirs. It was a two-edged weapon; before the victims died, they went through a period of sheer terror. You used distilled ginger with some drug that enabled you to control the paralysis that precedes death from jake-leg... and in the inexplicable uniformity of that paralysis, lay your hold over your victims.

"I'll wager you first met Virginia Wilder when she contacted you to do away with her husband. And that his death was the first. You accomplished it by ordinary means—deliberately—so that police might think they had a case. After that, you saw your chance to let your brother take the blame, with you and your exonerated woman friend free. Then, none of your other murders would have seemed unsolved. I have only Virginia Wilder's word that her husband died as your other victims died—the word of a murderess trying to frame an innocent man."

White's face went livid. "You've told them about Virginia," he said.

By all rights, that should have been the end of the Bleeder. But Nat Perry was no longer in front of the desk when the bullet landed. He was on his stomach, skidding across the floor toward White. His powerful, trained fingers twisted around the man's ankles, and jerked. White grunted—it happened too quickly for a louder protest—and fell backwards. Then Perry was on him.

"John!" It was a woman's voice at the doorway, and there were men's fists rapping against the door Perry had chained shut. "John, don't try any more—"

Virginia Wilder's voice. A voice utterly hopeless, lost beyond redemption, but to the man Perry was fighting it was like a command. He went limp. As Perry stood away from him, he came shakily to his feet. "You win," he said, in a ghost-tone. "Better open the door."

O'Connor was there, and his prisoner, the prisoner who would not escape again. She lifted her hands to John White, and he took her in his arms.... Perry didn't stay to see what happened after that.

It was cooler on Charles Street when he went out. A child had been killed on that corner; the red stain was still visible. As he remembered the child, all those waves of revulsion he had fought down earlier rose in Perry.

"Caught 'em, didn't they?" said the patrolman, with satisfaction.

"Yes," said Perry. "Yes, they caught 'em." Caught what? Virginia Wilder's poignant and evil beauty, that would leave this world a darker place for having existed in it? Would anything they did to those two people in the apartment upstairs bring back the life of a dead child?

"Hell," he said to the cop. "I ought to be sorry. It's costing me five thousand dollars."

SECRET STREET

BY EJLER JAKOBSON

THE LIFE OF *Giacomo Matteo began in the crooked streets of the humbler part of Genoa, Italy, and it would never again, he knew, wander too far away. No farther than Via Garibaldi and the Church of the Annunziata. Giacomo had done his share of traveling; he had seen his bit of the world. In this white edifice, some day soon, the blessed saints would take his immortal soul and all its secrets, while that part of old Giacomo with which the world was as familiar as it cared to be, would be put away forever—and small loss, too. He was just an old man, a poor man in a poor part of the world—known to hardly anyone except the birds of the Annunziata. As they once had upon Saint John the Baptist, the church doves descended upon Giacomo in droves as he came each day to look at the church and feed them.*

The bird man with his doves—and his secrets....

In a cheap west-side hotel in uptown New York, Detective August Meyer gazed upon a scene of violence and reflected on all the ways there were to make a living. Of them all, his was not the most pleasant. Other people met girls like this when they were at their prettiest—at dances, at parties, or for a quiet evening at home. He was seeing this girl at her worst. Not that Emmeline Ferris cared any more.

She was quite dead.

She was blonde, young, and strangely beautiful. There was a curious frailty about her and a strength, too; and it seemed to Detective Meyer that she was one for whom life might have held a lot of promise. One, too, who had lived beyond her years. But for some reason or other, he couldn't escape the notion that she might have been starting on a new and vital enterprise if death had not interrupted her. There was a curious peace about her in this violence her murderer had created.

He asked his routine questions. The management knew little about her, except that she had been a model tenant and came from London. When the house physician had treated her for a minor ailment, she had told him she was to be married as soon as her fiance arrived from England. So that, Meyer thought, was her reason for looking as if her life were just beginning. And then he found the dead part of her life, the part that had added age to her years, and that had died before Emmeline Ferris actually did.

Tucked away under some old clothing, he uncovered a small, diamond-encrusted hypodermic case, whose expensive glamour contrasted strangely with her currently seedy surroundings.

He looked sharply at the girl on the bed—a dope addict. But there were no marks of the needle now. *Cured,* he thought.

He examined the case carefully and got another surprise. Painted on the inside bottom with exquisite detail and workmanship was a picture of a white church and an old man feeding the church doves. The painting bore the dead girl's signature….

Old Giacomo wandered out of the ancient shadows of the crooked streets into the sunlight of the little white church, and the white doves descended upon him like so many welcoming holy spirits. But they were not yet ready to take the soul of Giacomo, so he fed them, not guessing that back in New York, raw and cold in the grip of an early spring gale, Detective Meyer was staring intently at his picture, wondering who he was and where. Wondering and speculating about the name of the bird man….

Art galleries had not heard of Emmeline Ferris, whose great talent apparently had been overwhelmed by her narcotic habit. The perfect little miniature on the inside bottom of the narcotic case seemed almost symbolic to Detective Meyer as he closed the box and set about checking more prosaic clues to her murderer.

But there were none. Evidently Emmeline Ferris had done a thorough job of breaking off with her old life; among her effects there was not the slightest clue to anyone who might have known her, not even to her alleged fiance. Then, several days later, a letter arrived from the young man in London, saying he would be over any day now to marry her, and "—God be good to us." It was signed Dudley Ash.

Three hours after Detective Meyer had cabled Scotland Yard for information concerning Dudley Ash, he received a reply.

Ash had been murdered in his bedroom almost at the same moment his fiance had been killed three thousand miles away in New York!

New York and Scotland Yard burned up the ether, swapping information, and got exactly nowhere. Ash had been an art dealer—and there were no clues to his killers. There simply was no reason why either of the two young people should have been slain.

Gradually the case lapsed into the files of the unsolved killings of two continents. Detective Meyer was taken off it and put to other work. After all, taxpayers were still getting knocked off, and the survivors insisted he earn his keep.

In due time and some promotions later, when the case of Emmeline Ferris had been forgotten, he was sent to Europe on an assignment. The job took him to Genoa and Via Garibaldi, and he had a sudden, strange sensation that he had been here before. There was a white church....

On that day again Giacomo Matteo came to see if the spirits of Annunziata were ready to receive him. Again they descended upon him in clouds, and again in their shiny eyes he read only friendliness and simple hunger for his bread crumbs. Nothing more....

Across the street an American cop grabbed the nearest passerby and managed to make himself understood. Who was the old man feeding the birds? The other shrugged himself free, stared at the demented foreigner.

"Who cares—he does that every day. The bird man, they call him."

A police interpreter proved of even less value. Giacomo Matteo refused to talk. He had had nothing to do with the police, even though he had lived many years on the crooked, shady streets of Genoa. He had done nothing.

Meyer sent to New York for the diamond-encrusted narcotic case, and when it arrived, showed it to Giacomo Matteo. The old man's eyes softened when he saw the painting.

"She was good...."

"She's dead—murdered," Meyer interrupted him.

The old man's eyes widened; then words poured from him in a

torrent. "So they got her at last—she lived on my street, where she was like many others...."

Emmeline Ferris had been the Genoa agent of an English dope-smuggling ring—her own addiction had made her useful to the gang as bait to lure others. It was thus she had met Dudley Ash, who had persuaded her to break away from both narcotics and her gang. Old Matteo had helped the couple to escape. Now from Matteo's lips came names and dates—enough to break one of Europe's greatest narcotics setups, involving even a British peer in its sordid clutches.

The head of the ring, one Hugh Harkness, was captured in Switzerland. He was hanged in London, officially for the murder of Dudley Ash, but also, in the private books of Detective Meyer, for the death of Emmeline Ferris.

And when old Matteo went to visit once more the doves of Annunziata, it seemed they were a little more ready to receive him this time....

COFFIN FOR A BATHING BEAUTY

BY EJLER JAKOBSON

"**I HAVE** come back, my dear," Mr. Williams probably said, "to turn back the clock." Perhaps he smiled affectionately down at her brimming eyes, wondering what the effect would have been if he had told her, *I've come back to kill you!* For Mr. Williams had a sense of humor.

Perhaps his wife nuzzled his lapel—nobody knows exactly, for there are sacred moments in every woman's life and you're a cad if you insist on all the details. Perhaps she only said, "I've missed you, Henry."

Henry, unfortunately, hadn't missed *her* for the two years he had been away from home. He hadn't missed anything about her—except her comfortable cash income and her bank balance.

He had come home silk-hatted, soft-spoken, looking reasonably prosperous, as a man of forty should. He fully intended, as he had given her to understand, to make the rest of her days happy ones. But it would not, he had already decided, be a long, hard pull.

He proceeded to give her all the comforts of home. A house on High Street, Herne Bay—this was England. He made out a will in her favor. She, of course, reciprocated. He insisted she have a medical check-up and even took the doctor aside and told him what he said she would be too embarrassed to mention—Beatrice was subject to periodic fits or seizures. He bought her a bathtub....

For this, only a few days later, he was bitterly blaming himself, right out loud. Stiff and cold in the bathtub, lay his beloved wife, who had evidently been taken with one of her seizures just as she was reaching for the soap—a nice little human touch, that.

Mr. Williams went to Southsea to recuperate. He changed back to his real name, George Joseph Smith, to be anonymously alone with his sorrow—although not too alone. There was a pretty little nurse, who also happened to be an heiress.

Alice Burnham was her name. Just a few months after his first wife's death, Mr. Smith decided to bestow his spare name upon her, after prevailing upon her to insure herself for a few thousand in his favor.

Alice wrote to papa, a retired merchant, who sent his blessings—plus enough money for Alice to draw up a respectable will in George's favor, as he had done in hers. By this time the couple were wed—and forty-eight hours later Alice lay dead in her bathtub, evidently the victim of a periodic ailment, whose presence Mr. Smith had previously confided to a local doctor.

Just to prove that some things come in threes, a year later found George Joseph Smith wedded once more, this time to one Margaret Elizabeth Lofty, in London, who commanded a slightly higher insurance value than had her predecessors—and was just as bad a risk. She, too, proved highly susceptible to death by drowning in a bathtub.

Mr. Smith probably would have continued his homicidal hobby indefinitely if it hadn't been for a Mr. Crossley in Blackpool. This gentleman noted the two accounts of the demises of Mr. Smith's wives in the newspaper obituary columns and sent both clippings to Scotland Yard, with marginal notations pointing out certain parallelisms.

They strung up Mr. Smith on an unlucky day, August 13, 1915. He reacted to the rope just like any other mortal, though his record as a bathtub murderer has never been equaled.

As far as anybody knows, nobody has successfully gotten rid of even a single wife via the bathtub ever since.

DOUBLE LIFE OF A PHONEY

BY EJLER JAKOBSON

IN MISCOLKZ, HUNGARY, a few years before the war, was a small food shop. When you went in, you were served as a peasant is served by royalty. If you were insulted, you went away and they did not miss you—neither the proprietor nor the customers. But if you had that unusual talent for understanding which is reserved for children and specially gifted adults, you would realize that you were at a way station on that rainbow trail to the pot of gold which most of us never take. You would discover that you suddenly believed in a concept only slightly less fantastic than the fourth dimension—namely, that you only live twice!

The chances are that you tossed away the dishonest dreams of youth long ago and settled down to living just once. If you did, you were lucky. Living your two lives to the full takes it out of a man— Ignatz Strassnoff, the proprietor of the little food shop, could have told you that. Of humble origin, he made a swindler's reality of make-believe, became the consort of princes and bishops, and even applied himself once, briefly, to tampering with the course of history.

It all began, appropriately enough, on the stage, some time before the turn of the century. Stassnoff, a young actor then, played the part of an Imperial Hussar in a forgotten play. The resplendent uniform clothed more than his body, it clothed his thoughts and his brain. It *made* him a Hussar of noble birth, and he knew, long before the play wound to its tedious, artificial end, that no stage would ever hold him.

So, when the silly drama was over, it was only natural that he shouldn't remove his costume. He had needed no make-up for his part, so he did not pause to remove it. He simply walked out of the stage door and into the night, to stroll for a moment under the moon and gradually witness, within himself, the metamorphosis of a dream into reality.

The next day, make-believe soldier Stassnoff walked into the ornate offices of the supplier of uniforms for the Imperial Hussars. Presenting the compliments of his commanding officer, a high army dignitary, he demanded an immediate estimate on a large order of new dress uniforms the cavalry needed before an impending review by the Emperor himself.

Hussar Strassnoff was haughty and courtly and cynical of mien, a most realistic job. In a very short while he proved himself corruptibly human. He took the bedazzled military tailor aside and confessed he had been authorized to pay 8,000 kronen in excess of the cited value of the uniforms—a sum he was willing to split equally with the firm supplying the goods, provided he could have his share in cash immediately. Pressing financial obligations, this military facsimile confessed with a noble wink—and shortly walked out of the place with a wallet bulging comfortably with the crown's money.

A thing that wasn't so—sired by why-not out of might-have-been—this will o' the wisp in cavalry pants made his rounds, feeding on things that shouldn't have been. Patriotically he arranged for fodder for cavalry horses and new, fine equipment for the men of war, removing fantastic sums of graft from circulation.

Then Ignatz Strassnoff woke up—in irons. Nor did he dream again for nearly two years, not until he finally got out of jail.

Then he found himself working on a progressive newspaper, whose publisher, Zoltan Karlitz, was a practical idealist believing in political reform and striving to reach his goal by getting himself elected to the parliament. For some time Ignatz Strassnoff, who walked the rainbow trail as easily as he trod the pavements of Budapest, watched his employer's newspaper campaign with detached interest. No group idealist himself, he decided Karlitz's aims were solid. He knew, too, that Karlitz stood not a chance of being elected, with the local moneyed interests forming a solid front against him.

Great numbers of voters were being given no time to get to the polls by their employers. The situation was made to order for the whimsical talents of Strassnoff.

HE WAITED until the night of the election. Then he casually picked up the nearest telephone and quietly called Budapest's leading firms. It was the Minister of Commerce speaking. The government was grateful for the support given its candidates, whom the day's voting had assured of re-election. It would be a handsome gesture if the residue of the population were allowed to go to the polls now that it could do no harm....

Budapest awoke the following morning to a hilarious practical joke—Karlitz had been elected by a slim but decisive margin!

The irrepressible Strassnoff went along to parliament as his confidential secretary, and continued to reach for the pot o' gold. With characteristic facility he ceased being Strassnoff and became Karlitz—especially when it came to signing checks. The disillusioned Karlitz had him sent to the most formidable jail in Hungary, where for three years Strassnoff enjoyed complete national obscurity. He came out of this prison a profoundly reformed character.

Along with a female companion of some of his earlier peccadilloes, he became a regular churchgoer—and soon knew the most intimate details of the private lives of the important members of the religious hierarchy.

Going over his many notes, it seemed to him that, as soon as continue to be Ignatz Strassnoff, he might as well—at least occasionally—be the eminent Councilor von Zahranyi.

Arraying himself in the proper regalia, Strassnoff called upon the aged Bishop of Neutra, the real Zahranyi's uncle. When the old man failed to recognize him as a nephew, Strassnoff blandly convinced the bishop that His Eminence's mind was failing and sadly revealed that it was his duty to report the true state of affairs at Budapest—unless, of course, the bishop were willing to come across with a sizable portion of his cash assets.

The bishop promptly recognized him as a kinsman and paid him!

Encouraged, Strassnoff investigated further and discovered that the high clerics of Central Europe were as amenable to paying graft to save their jobs as had been the more mundane office-holders. One haul, involving the Bishop of Steinamanger, netted him fifty thousand of the best—and led to his downfall.

Arrested, Strassnoff attempted to make a clean breast of things by confessing to his earlier mulcting of His Eminence of Neutra—and was amazed to find that that dignitary held steadfast to the story that the real von Zahranyi had visited him and that any financial transactions between uncle and nephew were nobody's business. Strassnoff's confession reacted against him at the trial. It was considered to be an effort to blacken the Church's name unnecessarily.

His conviction put an end to his triumphs. When he came out again, he had little heart left for more.

Strassnoff retired to the dingy little shop in Miskolcz. It might have been the pot of gold Strassnoff spent a lifetime searching for. He got it for nothing—it was subscribed and presented to him by well-wishers who had enjoyed his tripping of the pompous. He had his honest friends, this swindler who trod his rainbows, and who inadvertently did as much as any single man to strip the middle Europe of the Hapsburgs of its shame and hypocrises.

But he couldn't settle down. The shop went to ruin while the old man tried vainly to capitalize on his previous audacities by putting them on the stage. You walk the same rainbow only once—and when he finally died in poverty in the early thirties, almost the only possession he left behind was an old actor's uniform of the Hussars.

www.ingramcontent.com/pod-product-compliance
Lightning Source LLC
Chambersburg PA
CBHW070938250626
47159CB00009B/3304